Outbreak

*Also by Chris Ryan, and published by
Random House Children's Books:*

The Code Red Adventures
FLASH FLOOD
WILDFIRE

The Alpha Force Series
SURVIVAL
RAT-CATCHER
DESERT PURSUIT
HOSTAGE
RED CENTRE
HUNTED
BLOOD MONEY
FAULT LINE
BLACK GOLD
UNTOUCHABLE

*Adult thrillers also available, published by the
Random House Group; see www.rbooks.co.uk*

Outbreak

A CODE RED ADVENTURE

CHRIS RYAN

DOUBLEDAY

OUTBREAK
A DOUBLEDAY BOOK 978 0 385 61289 0
978 0 385 61290 6 (trade paperback)

Published in Great Britain by Doubleday,
an imprint of Random House Children's Books
A Random House Group Company

This edition published 2007

1 3 5 7 9 10 8 6 4 2

The Random House Group Limited makes every effort to ensure that the papers used in
its books are made from trees that have been legally sourced from well-managed and
credibly certified forests. Our paper procurement policy can be found at:
www.randomhouse.co.uk/paper.htm

Mixed Sources
Product group from well-managed
forests and other controlled sources
www.fsc.org   Cert no. TT-COC-2139
FSC   © 1996 Forest Stewardship Council

Set in 13.5/17.5 Garamond by
Falcon Oast Graphic Art Ltd.

RANDOM HOUSE CHILDREN'S BOOKS
61–63 Uxbridge Road, London W5 5SA

www.kidsatrandomhouse.co.uk
www.rbooks.co.uk

Addresses for companies within The Random House Group Limited can be found at:
www.randomhouse.co.uk/offices.htm

THE RANDOM HOUSE GROUP Limited Reg. No. 954009

A CIP catalogue record for this book is available from the British Library.

Printed and bound in Great Britain
by Clays Ltd, St Ives plc

A CODE RED ADVENTURE

Location: Democratic Republic of Congo

PROLOGUE

A small village in the east of the Democratic Republic of Congo, not far from the Rwandan border. Just before midnight.

They would be dead by morning. When you've seen it happen enough times, you get used to the signs.

Naked apart from an old pair of underpants, he lay listlessly on the elderly, stained mattress, its springs broken and its stuffing now home to a thousand invisible bugs. By the dim, smoky light of a candle, she watched his chest rise and fall in time with his heavy, laboured breathing. It seemed somehow too big for the rest of his emaciated body. He had not eaten for eight days, not since he fell ill. And he hadn't eaten much even before that: he was a poor man.

Beside him on the mattress lay his wife. Her body, heavier than her husband's, was covered with a piece of material that had once been colourful but was now ragged and dirty. Her breathing was forced too. Rasping. Occasionally her eyes would open and roll around, unseeing, in their sockets, before closing again. Now and then she would shout out, but it was impossible to understand what she was saying.

She sounded frightened, though.

Her left hand lay lightly against her husband's arm; but like his, it didn't move. The unmistakable buzz of a mosquito hummed around them, explaining the angry welts that covered their skin. And despite the hot humidity of the night air, they did not sweat. Their bodies were too dehydrated for that.

A young girl, no more than fourteen, walked across the dusty floor of the hut with an earthenware cup of water in her hands. Gently she dipped her fingers into it, then brushed the moistness against the cracked lips of her two patients. The man's tongue, furred and leathery, moved slightly towards the wetness, but in the end it seemed like too much effort and it fell back into the hollow of his mouth, giving his tired face an even more spectral appearance. Her wide eyes gazed at them, then she sighed and stepped back to the small wooden stool from which she had nursed them ever since they had become too weak to stand up.

The girl spoke five languages: French, three dialects of Bantu, and even some English. And in all of them she had repeated the same words over the past few days more times than she could count. '*Mama, Papa, please do not die.*'

But she knew it was a vain hope. She had seen villagers die of malaria before, driven to madness by their feverish hallucinations, and she muttered a silent prayer of thanks that her parents had, at least, been spared that. It had been the same for the two other families who had been hit by the disease in recent days: quick, virulent. Malaria was a constant presence in the life of these villagers, and the girl had learned enough about it in her short life to know that it came in different forms. But she had never seen it this bad before.

Perhaps that was why there were others in the village who thought there was something more sinister at work.

It had been a year since the mine on the edge of the village had been opened. Originally they had hoped to be digging for tin, but the boss men had found something else down there. Something valuable. It had made some in the village nervous. They knew that the ground was sacred to the village ancestors, being the final resting place of the tribal elders for as long as their people had been in these parts. They knew that great harm would befall those who disturbed it. But the lure of the money had been too great.

Her father had worked hard all his life. When the mine-owners came, he was offered three times his normal pay to work for them – enough to make him forget about tribal superstitions, or at least put them to a far corner of his mind. Many other workers in the village had made the same decision, although most of them carried magical objects somewhere about their bodies to protect them from ancient evils. And now three of them had succumbed to this horrific illness, as had various members of their families. The tribal elders, who had been so keen to welcome the mine-owners into the village in the first place, had ordered an X to be marked in thick, red paint on the corrugated-iron doors of their dwellings – so that the villagers could identify the cursed houses, and stay away.

But the superstitions were not enough to keep men from going down the mine. Poverty and war had killed so many in this part of the world for so long that death was a common occurrence, more likely to come upon you if you had no money. And money was what the mine was all about.

The girl put all these thoughts from her head. It wasn't that she didn't believe in the malevolent powers of the ancestors; it was just that all she could think about was that her parents were at death's door, and she had to look after them.

But not for long. As the first light of dawn eased the village and the dense jungle that surrounded it out of darkness, her father drew his last breath. He exhaled as though he was breathing his spirit out of his body. Five minutes later, her mother too slipped silently away.

The girl had expected to cry when it happened, but now the moment was upon her, she found she could not. She just sat on that little wooden stool and looked at them, her mind a confusion of memories.

And then she stood up and walked out of the tiny hut. A small group of villagers had congregated at the end of her ramshackle street, looking out onto a stark clearing. They were safely outside the ring of protective symbols that had been crudely drawn in the dusty earth. How long they had been there the girl did not know – all night, probably – but now they watched her expectantly, not daring to draw near to the house that had fallen under this terrible curse for fear of bringing it upon themselves – just like the girl's father had done upon her mother, and upon the girl herself, for all they knew.

She stood up straight and, in a clear voice, spoke in Kikongo, the language of the region. 'They have departed.'

The bystanders looked fearfully at each other, then melted away, no doubt to spread the news around the village. The girl knew what they would be saying, knew the rumour that would be spreading round the population like a contagious infection. She half believed it herself. 'The curse of the ancestors has not been lifted,' the villagers would be muttering. 'Halima's parents are dead. We told you it would be so . . .'

CHAPTER ONE

Kinshasa International Airport. Four weeks later.

'You have money?'

Russell Tracey and his son Ben looked nervously at the sinewy man in front of them who held their bags as though they weighed next to nothing. Ben had always quietly assumed that he was stronger than most of his friends, but even he had had trouble lifting his dad's heavy suitcase onto the check-in belt at Heathrow when they had started their journey more than twenty hours ago. Now this tough Congolese man, his skin a deep, ebony black and his close-cropped hair flecked with grey, had made him doubt himself.

'Um ... I'm not sure what you mean,' Russell

stuttered slightly, his northern accent sounding peculiarly out of place in the stark, basic surroundings of the airport. His eyes flicked down at Ben, and then back at the man who had already told them, in a gruff, unfriendly voice, that his name was Abele. A flash of a dog-eared identification card bearing the logo of the Eastern Congo Mining Corporation had told them that this was indeed the person they had been expecting to meet them.

It had been a real relief when they had heard Abele's deep and harshly accented voice calling their names out of the crowd. Within moments of stepping onto the airport concourse, they had been surrounded by a crowd of young Congolese, not much older than Ben, all jostling to try and carry their bags in return for payment. Russell had tried to tell them as politely as he could that their services weren't required; but his politeness had been met with indifference at best, aggressiveness at worst. One of their unwanted porters, older than the others and with a nasty glint in his eye, had started to argue with him. His English wasn't good enough for them to understand what he was saying, but the tone of his voice left them in no doubt that he was unimpressed that they were declining his offer of help. Ben's dad had instinctively placed himself between his son and the crowd of people who had gathered round to witness the argument, stuttering politely in English in an attempt to defuse the situation. So when they heard their names being called, he had let out an audible breath of relief.

It took a few harsh words from Abele in a language they didn't understand for the vultures to disappear and swoop on some other unsuspecting new arrival, though these were few and far between by now. But it seemed like this Abele wanted their money too.

He turned and started carrying their luggage towards the exit, with Ben and his dad trotting nervously along, one on either side. 'If you have money, take it out of your wallet. Leave only' – the Congolese thought for a moment – 'four hundred francs.'

They stepped through the automatic doors into the oppressive morning heat as Ben performed a quick calculation in his head. Four hundred francs – about fifty pence. He had forty pounds in his wallet, and travellers' cheques on top of that. Where was he supposed to put the rest of his money if not there? As if echoing his question, his dad spoke. 'What should we do with the rest of it?'

Abele continued walking along a poorly maintained road towards a group of cars. 'Put it in your shoes,' he said bluntly.

'I see,' Russell said earnestly. 'Well, if you think it's sensible . . .' and he removed his wallet from inside his light linen jacket. Beads of sweat were already forming on the bald part of his head.

'Not here!' Abele snapped, looking around to check that nobody had seen, then flashing Russell an impatient look. 'Wait until the car.' He strode on in silence.

The vehicle to which he led them looked as though it had seen better days. The green and orange stripes along the bonnet suggested it was – or had once been – a taxi, but if that was the case it was like no taxi Ben had ever seen. There were dents all over the side that was facing them, and patches of rust had entirely eaten their way through the metal. The rear bumper was hanging precariously at an angle. As Abele opened the boot, Ben was sure he caught sight of a large cockroach scurrying away from the sudden sunlight. He and his father climbed into the hard, uncomfortable back seat and both looked around for a non-existent seatbelt as Abele tried to turn the engine over. It took six choking coughs of the machinery before he managed to judder it into life, and as it did so, the inside of the car filled with the unmistakably greasy smell of petrol fumes. They jolted as Abele pulled out into the road and sped off, paying no attention to the fact that the rickety suspension made it feel more like a roller-coaster ride than a car.

Ben felt his brown combat trousers and white T-shirt start to cling to him in the heat. 'Why do we need to put our money in our shoes?' he asked, half out of a desire to break the uncomfortable silence that had descended on the car.

'*Voleurs*,' Abele spoke the word in his native French, and neither Ben nor his dad needed anyone to translate for them: robbers.

'Between here and Kinshasa, you think?' Russell asked lightly, sceptically almost, removing his wallet to act on Abele's instructions and giving Ben a nod that indicated he should do the same. 'We'll be safe in the car, surely?'

Abele smiled slightly, the first time he had done so since they had met, and displayed a full set of yellowing teeth.

'With you, I mean . . .' Ben's dad continued.

'In the Congo, Mr Tracey' – Abele spoke more slowly now, leisurely almost – 'the only person not at risk from *voleurs* is the man with no money.' He thought for a moment before continuing in a quieter voice, 'And even he is not safe.'

The car fell silent once again as Abele's passengers secreted their valuables in their shoes. Ben looked out of the window to try and divert his attention from the intolerable heat. The road was busy, and most of the cars were in a state of similar disrepair to Abele's, though occasionally there was something a bit more modern and in better condition. Occasionally they were passed by white minibuses filled with passengers – the bush taxis he had read about, Ben assumed.

After a while he almost managed to forget how fast Abele was travelling, and it came as something of a surprise when he slowed down rapidly. 'Checkpoint,' the black man muttered under his breath.

Ben and his dad exchanged a glance. 'Will we need our passports?' Russell asked.

Abele shook his head. 'No,' he muttered. 'Not passports.' His voice didn't encourage further questioning.

They crawled forwards, and it was five minutes before the checkpoint guards came into view. They wore khaki uniforms and grim expressions, and had ugly-looking AK-47s brandished under their arms. Some of the cars in the queue were waved through without question; others were held for longer before being allowed to go forward. Eventually it was their turn. A guard rapped harshly on Abele's closed window, and he opened it reluctantly. The guard peered in, looked at Ben and his father without emotion, then started talking to Abele. They spoke in deeply accented French that Ben could barely understand. Suddenly the guard turned his attention to the back seat and spoke slowly, more clearly. '*Mille francs, chaque personne*,' he instructed.

Ben glanced into the rear-view mirror. Abele was watching him, and he shook his head imperceptibly. Ben took his lead and pulled his wallet from his pocket. '*Je n'ai que quatre cent francs,*' he enunciated in his best French. *I only have four hundred francs.*

The guard looked at him suspiciously. 'Get out,' he said, reverting to English. Ben did as he was told. 'You too,' the guard told his dad, before turning back to Abele and saying, 'You, wait there.'

Ben and his dad stood uncomfortably together by the side of the car. One of Ben's hands brushed lightly against the metal, making him wince: it was piping hot. The guard snatched Ben's wallet from his hand and hungrily rifled through, pulling the few crumpled notes that had been stored away there and then handing it back. He gestured impatiently at Ben's dad, who also handed over his wallet, and was also relieved of his money. The cash in his hand, the guard visibly lost interest in his captives. '*Allez,*' he muttered before turning to the next car in line; but he stopped in his tracks when he heard Ben speak.

'What are we paying for?' he asked in a clear voice.

The guard looked back over his shoulder, a dangerous look on his face, then turned round to look at Ben. He licked his lips, and his right hand lightly touched the body of his AK-47 before he answered with a single word. 'Taxes.'

Ben was about to respond, when he heard his father interrupt. 'Just get back in the car, Ben,' he hissed. Another look at the face of the guard persuaded him that maybe his dad was right, and quickly the two of them got back inside and shut the doors behind them. Abele sped off.

Ben couldn't help feeling indignant at having been so blatantly stolen from, and at the same time he felt the heat of Abele's frequent glances in the smeared rear-view mirror. 'That wasn't taxes,' he burst out finally. 'Was it?'

Abele shrugged. 'I already told you, in the Congo the only man safe from *voleurs* is the man with no money.'

'But they were policemen, not robbers.'

'Then you should think yourself lucky, young Ben,' Abele intoned. 'If they were real' – he struggled with the English word – '*robbers*, you would not have got away without being searched. And if they had found more money in your shoe . . .' He put two fingers to his head to indicate a gun before making a clicking sound with his tongue.

'Then why on earth did you tell us to hide the money away?' Ben's dad asked, unable to hide his anger.

Abele shrugged again. 'On this road,' he said, 'you are probably safe from that kind of robber.' He thought for a minute, before adding, 'In the daytime, at least.'

They drove on in silence.

Ben felt the sickness of uncertainty in the pit of his stomach. Maybe his mum had been right – maybe he really shouldn't have come. The idea of Dr Bel Kelland, world-famous environmental activist, trying to ban her son from travelling to Africa had seemed pretty out of character, but she'd been adamant. The Democratic Republic of Congo was one of the most unstable places on earth, she had fumed, and she had been shocked that Ben's dad – or 'your father' as she would always disapprovingly refer to him – had even suggested that he accompany him on his business trip to the region.

'It's just too dangerous, Ben,' she had told him.

'More dangerous than Adelaide?' Ben had replied archly. It had only been a matter of months since the two of them had been caught at the centre of the terrible fires that had swept across the Australian city. A couple of weeks of his longed-for summer holiday spent exploring an exciting part of Africa would seem like a walk in the park compared to that, surely. It would take his dad a week at the most to complete his business, and then they would be free to do as they pleased. Russell had even suggested taking a flight to the holiday resorts of Kenya, and Ben was certainly up for that.

'Don't be flippant, Ben,' his mother had chided sharply, before changing tack a little and appealing to his reason. 'Look, love, I'm not going to ban you from going, but just think about it carefully, OK?'

'OK, Mum.'

He'd been as good as his word, reading up on the country that used to be known as Zaire on the Foreign Office's website. It made for pretty alarming reading, and the list of vaccinations he had needed was as long as his punctured arm. Back in England, though, the warnings had just been words on paper; now Abele's words had highlighted the fact that these were not just idle fears: this strange land in the middle of Africa was clearly a very dangerous place.

Bel had eventually become resigned to Ben's decision to go, but she had still been full of instructions. 'Don't forget to take clean water with you wherever you go; and make sure you and your father take your malaria tablets – before you leave *and* after you come back. It's very important, Ben. People die of malaria, in their millions. Its incubation period is between seven days and a month – chances are you wouldn't even know you'd got it till you were back in England.'

Ben was snapped out of his reverie by the sound of his dad and Abele in conversation – or rather his dad talking enthusiastically, and Abele listening quietly.

'I'm a scientist,' Russell was saying in that slightly monotone voice that he always seemed to lapse into when he started explaining about his work. 'A chemist, actually. Specializing in minerals and ores. The company I work for is in the business of examining naturally occurring ores and evaluating whether they are of a good enough standard for mining. The company you work for, as I'm sure you know, is currently mining tin in the east of your country, and they believe they have hit upon a rich vein of Coltan.'

'I would not know about that,' Abele muttered. 'I just run errands for the boss men.'

'Ah, well, it's a very interesting substance, Coltan . . .'

Ben's attention wandered again. He had heard his dad expound about the value of Coltan more times than he could count since it had been confirmed that he would be accompanying him on this work trip. Columbite tantalite – used to create tantalum, the magic ingredient in almost any electrical item you care to name. Without Coltan, there would be no mobile phones, no computer chips, no PlayStations. It sold for $100 a pound, and anyone who mined it would be rich. The DRC was one of the major producers in the world.

'The mine is in a village in the east of the country called Udok. Are you familiar with it?'

'Of course.' Ben could have been mistaken, but as Abele spoke he was looking at him in the mirror. He could have sworn he saw a tightening of the eyes, a look that was half suspicion, half fear. 'I would not travel to Udok if it were up to me,' he muttered.

'Why on earth not?'

Abele paused. When he answered, it was without much conviction, as though he was not saying everything he was thinking. 'That part of the country is very dangerous,' he explained. 'Many *voleurs* . . . And anyway,' he continued with a certain reluctance, 'it is not wise to disturb the land like that. No good can come of such things.'

Ben was about to quiz him further when he felt the car suddenly slow down again. The road had led them to what seemed to be a slightly more built-up area – the outskirts of Kinshasa, he assumed. 'Not another checkpoint?' he asked.

Abele shook his head. 'I don't think so.'

'Then why is everyone slowing down?'

For a moment Abele didn't answer. When he did, it was curt. 'Over there,' he said, pointing to something on the side of the road.

Ben squinted his eyes. There was something lying there in a disjointed heap. It was only after several seconds had passed that he realized what it was.

A human body.

It was raggedly clothed: what material there was appeared to have been ripped to shreds. The limbs seemed to be cruelly out of position, pointing in different directions that were never naturally intended. The head was facing away from the road, a fact for which Ben was profoundly grateful. 'Why doesn't someone do something?' he whispered, craning his neck to look back at the body as the car passed it.

'What is there to do?' Abele replied simply.

'Well . . .' Ben stuttered, 'he should be taken away. Buried. His family should be told . . .'

Abele laughed gently, but there was no humour in that laugh. 'In my country,' he explained, 'if you approach that body, you take responsibility for it. Nobody wants that.'

'But you can't just leave him there.'

'He won't be left,' Abele said gruffly. 'The wild animals will see to that. He will be gone in three days. Maybe four.'

Ben didn't know what to say.

'You are shocked,' Abele continued. 'And so you should be. My poor country is a shocking place. You are not in your safe England now, Ben Tracey. Remember that.'

Ben glanced in the mirror to see Abele peering back at him, his sharp, bright eyes seeming to glow in his black face. It made Ben distinctly uncomfortable.

He turned his head and looked out of the window once more as they made their way deeper into Kinshasa.

Chapter Two

Back in England, Ben had checked on the Internet what the Foreign Office had said about travel to the area. It had been pretty straightforward: don't do it. If you must, move around with caution. Stay away from crowds. Remain vigilant. But Ben had been determined to look past that and find out as much about the country as possible. He had learned that Kinshasa lay on the south side of the Congo river, directly opposite Brazzaville, capital of the Republic of the Congo – they were the only two capital cities in the world to be so situated. What came through most, though, was that the DRC, formerly known as Zaire, had been ravaged by civil war. Violence and unrest were everywhere. British citizens were advised not to travel to the east of the country towards the Rwandan border, and they were being told to exercise extreme caution even in Kinshasa.

The hotel where they were to stay formed a striking contrast to the shanty-town outskirts of the city through which they had driven. Ben had been shocked and a little unnerved by the sight of the rickety dwellings with corrugated-iron roofs and all manner of emaciated animals scratching around outside. The further towards the centre they drove, however, the more these poor places gave way to broad streets and imposing yet shabby buildings. It should have been impressive, but somehow it wasn't.

The hotel was no different – two great white buildings surrounding a couple of swimming pools and tables covered with coconut-fibre parasols; there was room here for hundreds of people, but it was practically deserted. Abele looked decidedly uncomfortable as he carried their bags all the way to the steps leading to the hotel reception, but he refused to come in. Ben could sense his embarrassment as his father pressed him to join them for a drink: he obviously just wanted to get away from this place, the domain of Kinshasa's rich, whoever they might be. 'This is not somewhere for me,' he finally muttered. 'I will meet you outside when you want to go out.' He walked away before turning his head back towards them. 'You don't go with anyone else,' he warned. 'Only me.'

They would only be staying here for one night, and when Ben saw the room he was to share with his dad, he was glad about that – although half of him wondered what the rest of his trip had in store, if this was the best hotel in the country. Two single beds with fraying sheets were pushed up against the wall, and there was a large fan on the ceiling between the beds. A switch on the wall was supposed to operate it, but it didn't. The small sink was coming away from the wall, and there was an overriding smell of stale tobacco and something Ben couldn't quite place. Food, probably. He washed his hands and face – something he had been wanting to do ever since seeing the dead body by the side of the road – then pulled on a clean T-shirt. He and his dad were ready to leave within ten minutes.

Russell Tracey was being employed by the Eastern Congo Mining Corporation, and he was keen to meet his clients as soon as possible to make arrangements for the rest of their stay. It was only a five-minute drive to the company's headquarters, a faceless modern building on an island in the centre of one of the city's broad boulevards. Ben was surprised to see stony-faced guards carrying heavy weapons flanking the doors, but they recognized Abele, and the trio were allowed to enter without questions or other hindrance. The reception room itself was deliciously cool, with white stone floors and a wooden desk behind which a uniformed man sat with an imperious expression, nothing in front of him other than an old-style telephone and a holster. Ben noticed that it was empty, and couldn't help wondering where the accompanying weapon was. Abele spoke to him in what Ben assumed to be Lingala, the Bantu dialect most prevalent in this part of the country – though in truth there was no way he could have known the difference between Lingala and Kikongo, which was spoken in the jungle regions further east – and the receptionist made a phone call. Abele turned to them, nodded speechlessly, then wandered off to a different part of the building while Ben and his dad were left waiting, unsure what to do.

They didn't have to wait for long, however. Within a minute a large white man burst through a set of double doors into the reception and walked towards Ben's dad with an outstretched hand and a broad, toothy smile on his face. He had a thick mane of black hair – suspiciously black, Ben thought, given that the lines on his face suggested he was at least sixty years of age. He grabbed Russell's hand and shook it firmly. 'Mr Tracey,' he almost bellowed in a tight South African accent. 'What a pleasure it is to have you here.'

'Likewise, Mr . . . ?'

'Kruger.' He smiled. 'Stefan Kruger.'

'Likewise, Mr Kruger.' Russell looked down at Ben. 'This is my son, Ben.'

Kruger appeared to notice Ben for the first time. He glanced at him, and the smile on his face seem to fail for a moment. 'You will be taking him to Udok?' he asked.

'That's right,' Ben's dad replied diffidently. 'They said it would be OK.'

Kruger appeared to consider that for a moment. Suddenly the grin reappeared on his face. 'Of course!' He wordlessly ruffled Ben's hair with his big hand. Ben said nothing.

'Come!' Kruger explained. 'We have plenty of people waiting to meet you, Mr Tracey. Ben, you want a Coke? There is a room to the side here where you can wait while the grown-ups do their work.'

Ben glanced up at his father. 'Um . . . actually,' Russell said politely, 'I was hoping Ben might join us. I'm sure he'll find it terribly interesti—'

'Rubbish!' Kruger shouted. 'Boring old grown-ups' stuff, eh, Ben?' He turned to the receptionist and said something in Lingala, his mock-friendliness suddenly falling away as he spoke to someone he clearly considered his inferior. 'Nkosana here will show you to the waiting place. We won't be long, eh, Mr Tracey?'

Ben's dad looked down at him apologetically and made as if to say something, but Ben spared him. 'It's all right, Dad. I'll wait.'

Russell Tracey nodded and followed Kruger out of the reception, while Nkosana stood up and unsmilingly gestured at Ben to follow him.

The room into which he was led was sparse. There were ten or fifteen chairs, and the Coke Ben had been promised was firmly imprisoned inside a vending machine that was not connected to the electricity. The steel-framed windows looked out onto the busy, car-filled boulevard. He looked around him, then turned to thank Nkosana, but when he did so the man was already gone. With a sigh, Ben strode over to the window and watched the cars go by. There was only so much interest to be had in doing that, however, so he pulled his mobile phone out of his pocket. There was no service, so he cranked up one of the games and started playing on that instead.

Ben had been in the room for perhaps forty-five minutes when the door opened. He looked up sharply to see a young woman walk in. She wore a colourful two-piece outfit and a headscarf that covered most of her hair but allowed a few tightly plaited strands to hang onto her long, shapely neck. She was perhaps eighteen years old, though it was difficult to say for sure, and she carried a metal bucket and a mop. The girl eyed Ben suspiciously as she entered; he just nodded curtly in return as she started to mop the floor slowly and, he thought, rather laboriously. All the while he felt her eyes on him, and he carried on playing on his phone more out of embarrassment than anything else.

Suddenly she spoke. 'You are one of the English?' she asked, her voice hesitant as she carefully enunciated the unfamiliar words.

Ben looked up from his phone and nodded.

'They say you travel to Udok tomorrow.'

'That's right,' Ben acknowledged. 'I'm Ben, by the way.'

'My name is Fatima. Udok is my village.'

Ben nodded, then watched as Fatima continued to mop the floor. Occasionally her eyes would flicker up to the door, and she would take a breath as if to say something, before thinking better of it. 'Do your family still live there?' Ben asked, more to persuade her to talk than anything else. 'In Udok, I mean.'

Immediately her eyes filled with tears as she nodded her head. 'Mr Ben,' she whispered, her voice low, 'I do not hear from them for many weeks. Each month I send them money, but I hear nothing. No letter, nothing.' Her voice became quieter, and she glanced once more at the door. 'I do not think the money reach them. My father work in the mine, but it is not enough.'

Ben smiled sympathetically, but he didn't know what to say. Suddenly the girl approached him with another conspiratorial glance at the door.

'Mr Ben,' she continued urgently, 'you do something for me. You find my sister, give her this.' She pulled something out of her pocket and pressed it into Ben's hand. He looked down to see a crumpled two-hundred-franc note. Twenty-five pence. And wrapped in the dog-eared note there was a small, roughly hewn piece of wood with a crude symbol etched into it, rather like an eye. Ben looked back up at Fatima, who was staring at him, the tears still brimming in her own wide, dark eyes.

Ben secreted the money and the wooden token away. 'How will I know your sister?' he asked.

'Her name is Halima,' Fatima said. 'She speak English very well, better than me. Ask in the village. They will know her.'

Ben nodded. 'I'll do what I can. When did you last go home?' he asked her gently.

Fatima looked down at the floor. 'It is not possible. If I leave to go home, then I lose this job. And then . . .' She left it hanging. There was a short silence before she continued. 'Mr Ben,' she said, her voice barely more than a whisper, 'it is many months since I am in Udok. When I left, it was very poor. Malaria a big problem. But now, I hear things.'

'What sort of things?'

'Bad things. The people here, they do not want me to know, but they cannot keep everything secret. People talk. It is the mine. It is, how do you say, *maudit*.'

Ben looked blankly at her. It was not a word he knew.

'The ancestors,' Fatima insisted. 'They say they have been—'

But suddenly Ben stopped the flow of her conversation by silently placing a hand on her arm; over her shoulder he had noticed someone standing quietly by the open door.

It was Kruger.

How long he had been there Ben couldn't tell, so intently had he been listening to Fatima; but for a moment all vestiges of that oily smile of his had been wiped from his face. As their eyes met, he started grinning once more, then strode purposefully towards them and pulled Fatima away by a rough tug on her shoulder. 'Excuse me, Ben,' he said with what came across as a strained politeness, then turned and started to admonish Fatima in that African dialect Ben could not understand. It wasn't necessary to know what the words meant, though: the harshness of his voice spoke volumes. When she was finally dismissed, Fatima scurried around collecting her cleaning things, then left without a word. 'She wasn't worrying you, I hope, eh, Ben?' Kruger asked, having lapsed back into his booming Afrikaans accent. He seemed a different person to the man who had been so abrupt with Fatima.

Ben shook his head.

'Good, I'm glad. Come with me.' They walked out of the room and Kruger led him along the corridor. 'You know what girls can be like, eh? Full of silly gossip. Especially girls like her – villagers. They don't know any better, eh?'

'Has my dad finished?' Ben tried to change the subject.

'Nearly finished, Ben. But there's been a change of plan. You'll be travelling to Udok later on today.'

'Today?' Ben was confused. 'I thought we were going tomorrow.'

'Like I say, a change of plan,' Kruger replied evasively. 'The plane has to fly this afternoon. Abele has been sent to collect your things from the hotel. He has' – Kruger smiled faintly to himself – 'volunteered to accompany you to the village.' They stopped outside an office in which three men were tapping away at old computers with boxy grey monitors. 'Wait here, Ben. Your dad will be along in a minute.' He walked off, leaving Ben loitering in the corridor.

Volunteered? Ben didn't like the way Kruger had said that. And it didn't make sense either. What was it Abele had said in the car just earlier that morning? '*I would not travel to Udok if it were up to me.*'

Ben felt into his pocket and wrapped his fingers round the crumpled note and the small wooden token Fatima had given him. He was beginning to think he might be of the same opinion . . .

CHAPTER THREE

Hundreds of miles away, a bat shrieked. It was a weak, pitiful sound.

The cave in which it lived was cool and perfectly dark, the water beneath it still and black. No light had found its way in here for millennia; no humans had tracked its existence, although lately they had come close. The bat was one of many thousands populating this hidden refuge; but in recent weeks their numbers had been declining.

Of late, the flight path of the bat had been erratic, and had become increasingly so in the past twenty-four hours. Occasionally its wing had scraped on the rough rock, causing it to shriek again, its panicked voice becoming lost in the echoing hubbub of the bats around him. Now and then it had flown blindly into one of its companions, causing a flurry of aggression from which it would fly away, knowing it could only come out worse.

Now, though, it lay on the floor. Its tiny abdomen made uneven attempts to breathe; its wings were spread on either side, occasionally twitching.

The bat gave one more call, though this would have been hardly audible even if it had not been drowned out by the cacophony of the colony. Then it twitched for a final time, before lying perfectly noiseless. Perfectly still.

And perfectly dead.

'Kruger said we were leaving this afternoon.'

It had taken Ben's dad about ten minutes to rejoin him, during which time he had hung around outside the office pondering the conversation he had had with Fatima. She had been cut off short, but clearly had wanted to tell him something. The look of fear on her face when Kruger had dismissed her suggested she would be unlikely to try again, though.

'It's *Mr* Kruger to you, Ben,' his dad said sternly.

'You wouldn't say that if you saw the way he just spoke to a cleaning lady I was talking to.' Ben knew he was answering back, but he calculated that he'd get away with it.

'There are cultural differences here, Ben. It's not up

to us to start judging the way people treat their staff. I'm sure the woman is glad just to have a job.'

'But don't you think it's a bit weird, us being packed off to Udok so quickly?'

'Of course not. A change of plan, that's all. I'm here on business, after all,' Russell said rather officiously. 'I need to be flexible for my clients.'

Ben replied with an unconvinced stare.

'Look, Ben,' his father continued, 'I know you were shaken up by what we saw earlier – the dead body and all. So was I. But we're in good hands. Mr Kruger is a very well-respected businessman and has a lot of influence in these parts. And Abele might be a bit gruff, but he seems . . . extremely competent.'

'But—'

'Ben! We are these people's guests. Come on, Abele is meeting us in reception and taking us to a local airfield.'

Sure enough, Abele was already there, surrounded by their luggage. He had no smile for them as they walked back into the reception; indeed he looked distinctly surly. Ben's dad approached with his arms spread out in a gesture of friendliness. 'Abele!' he said breezily. 'I understand you are accompanying us.'

Abele didn't reply, other than to flash them a dark look; he just picked up their luggage and started walking out of the building. They trotted behind.

The airfield to which they were travelling was about an hour outside Kinshasa, and the journey was thankfully uneventful, allowing Ben to watch the alien scenery through the window. Outside the city the road was poor, and Abele was forced to drive slowly; occasionally they would pass through a village, and the sight of a strange car – especially one containing two white faces – would provoke curious stares from the adults and invariably a horde of excited children, thin and poorly clothed, running after them.

The airfield itself was little more than a parched expanse of earth with an iron hut and a short, bumpy-looking runway. Waiting on the runway was a black and white twin-engined aircraft. Since Adelaide, where circumstances had forced him to fly a microlight over the burning city, Ben had made a study of such things, and he thought he recognized it as a Cessna 414. As they approached it, he became more sure he was right: the twin propellers, the long pointed nose – he'd be willing to bet money on it. He'd been wondering what sort of plane would be taking them to the village of Udok – there weren't many light aircraft that had the necessary range, but the Cessna was one of them. He felt a thrill of excitement that for a moment made him forget the worries that had been buzzing in his head; he was *really* looking forward to going up in this thing.

Abele parked the car by the metal shed and they all got out. A smiling man approached them and introduced himself as the pilot: Ben and his dad shook hands, but Abele seemed unwilling to speak, simply going about his usual business of carrying their bags across to the plane. Along with the pilot he lifted the bags up into the cabin; Ben and his dad walked up the steps, took their seats, and before they knew it the engines were humming, the propellers were spinning and they were trundling their way at increasing speed down the runway. Ben's eyes darted between the instruments on the control panel and the view out of the window: suddenly the jolting that shook them around in their seats was replaced by the familiar lurch in the stomach and that curious sense of weightlessness as the plane smoothly rose into the air. There was not a cloud in the sky here in the heart of Africa; there was unlikely to be any turbulence today. Ben found his eyes transfixed by the disappearing ground: the parched earth of the airfield soon gave way to a patchwork of browns and yellows, punctuated in the distance by the sparkling blue of the River Congo and the liver-shaped delta on which Kinshasa and Brazzaville lay. He was transfixed by the sight for some minutes, before the plane stopped climbing and settled into its steady flight.

The passengers sat in silence – Dad reading a book next to him, Abele sitting opposite, looking fiercely out of the window. Ben decided to ask the Congolese man the question that had been on his mind ever since his conversation with Fatima. 'Abele,' he said, 'why did you say you didn't want to travel to Udok?'

Abele's forehead creased into a frown. 'It doesn't matter,' he replied. His eyes flickered over at Ben, then looked sharply away again when he realized he was staring straight at him. Almost involuntarily, the black man's fingers brushed against a necklace he was wearing. Ben hadn't noticed it before: a piece of black leather, with a shiny triangle of metal and what looked like an etching he recognized upon it. It was an eye – one not a million miles away from the token Fatima had given him only a couple of hours ago. Ben felt a sudden coolness in his blood as Abele hid the necklace under his clothes, having realized that Ben had been gazing at it.

'What was that?' Ben asked quietly.

Abele shook his head. 'Nothing.'

'You weren't wearing it this morning.'

'Ben,' his dad chided.

Ben fell silent, but did not stop looking at Abele, who seemed to be deliberating whether or not to say something. Finally, it appeared, he could not help himself. 'It is a charm,' he said in a low voice. 'To protect against evil. If you were wise, you would wear one yourself.'

'That's enough, Abele.' Ben's father was uncharacteristically firm, but his face had a look of gentle amusement about it – his scientist's mind would not tolerate such superstitious talk, Ben realized. 'You'll frighten the lad.'

But I'm not frightened, Ben thought to himself, as Abele looked resolutely out of the window once more. Just intrigued. He thought back to what Fatima had said. There was something she had been trying to tell him, something she did not have good enough English to say. What was the word she used? *Maudit.* The village was *maudit.*

In his bag, Ben had a pocket French dictionary, ready to help him when his own schoolboy knowledge of French let him down. Wordlessly he opened the zip, rummaged around and pulled it out. The type was small, difficult to read in the vibrating plane, but as he diligently thumbed through the lists of unfamiliar words, he eventually found it.

Maudit.

It meant 'cursed'.

As the plane sped across the skies of central Africa, four men met in a plush room in the middle of Kinshasa. There was air conditioning and a carpet, and a bottle of Scotch whisky on the large mahogany meeting table. Two of the men were black, two of them white. They all wore suits and sipped their drinks from heavy tumblers. They didn't speak, but rather seemed to be waiting for someone.

Eventually that someone came – another white man with thick black hair and a lined face. He nodded at each of the others in turn before taking his seat at the table. 'You are all aware of what is happening?' he asked in a marked South African accent.

One of the black men spoke. He was short, with chubby features and a sing-song voice in which he spoke immaculately polite English. 'I think it would be best, my friend, if you filled us all in from the beginning.'

The South African nodded. 'Certainly, Mr Ngomo. As major shareholders, you will all be aware that the Eastern Congo Mining Corporation has been mining for tin in the east of the country for just over a year. Profits have been' – he shrugged – 'adequate.'

The men round the table nodded their heads.

'A little over six weeks ago, our mine manager there extended the excavations and believes he has come across a source of Coltan. Very plentiful, and on first examination of very high quality. I know a number of you have interests in other Coltan plants, so I needn't explain how lucrative it can be.'

'That rather depends,' one of the other white men interrupted, 'on the quality of the ore.'

'Indeed. As we speak, we have a British scientist flying out there to examine what we have found. He's one of the best.'

The men around the table nodded their approval.

'There is, however,' the South African continued, 'as you know, one small hitch.'

None of the men around the table looked at each other, and there was an oppressive silence before Mr Ngomo spoke. 'I assume you are referring to the unfortunate deaths of the mine-workers in recent weeks.'

The South African nodded almost serenely.

'Correct me if I'm wrong,' Ngomo continued, 'but the symptoms sound very much like those of extreme malaria.'

The South African inclined his head. 'Similar enough, I would say, for our purposes at least. Of course, there are rumours among the villagers . . .'

'Rumours are fine. They will keep people away. I understand that the village is extremely isolated, and that it seldom attracts visitors from the surrounding area. But if word gets out that we have discovered Coltan here, we can expect unwanted interest – you know how unstable that region is. I assume you have taken steps to stop word leaking out.'

'Of course,' the South African stated. 'Our mine manager controls all the transport in the village, and we have stopped any mail or deliveries from coming in or out. But I'm afraid there is an unforeseen problem.'

'What is that?'

'The workforce. They are dying more quickly than we anticipated. We don't have enough men or boys to work the mine.'

'Then you will need to bring in more personnel. Where is the nearest village?'

'Half a day's drive away.'

'We must import more workers from there. But we *must* keep it a secret, what we're doing.'

Suddenly one of the other white men spoke. 'If it's secrecy you want,' he observed, 'then I'm afraid it is already compromised.'

'What do you mean?'

'I mean the scientist. He will return to the outside world soon enough; and what if *he* suspects what *we* suspect about the deaths among the mine-workers and their families?'

The South African smiled blandly. 'His work will be done in a matter of days,' he observed before standing up and looking out of the window into a neat courtyard below. 'Unfortunately he has his son with him.' The men around him looked troubled.

'He's an unprepossessing kid – I don't think he will cause us any trouble. But I caught him speaking to one of the villagers who works in our offices.'

'She told him the rumours?' Nkomo asked.

'I don't know. But it's OK – I have arranged for them to travel to Udok earlier than expected. That way, we don't risk anybody else filling their heads with ideas. And of course, people succumb to all sorts of things in that part of the Congo.'

He turned round and gave everyone in the room a knowing look, which they returned in unified silence.

'Then I suggest' – Nkomo spoke in a monotone voice – 'that once the scientist has done his job, he and his son are considered entirely dispensable.'

Everyone in the room nodded their heads slowly.

'Good,' Nkomo continued smoothly. 'Then I think that just about concludes our business. Thank you for keeping us informed, Mr Kruger. You have been most helpful.'

Chapter Four

The Cessna started losing height.

Since Abele's mysterious warning, there had been almost no conversation in the cabin, and Ben had resorted to gazing aimlessly out of the window and watching the vastness of Africa pass beneath him. From that height it was difficult to make out the landscape over which they were flying, but as they prepared for landing, he found himself able to make out more distinct features: the thick canopy of jungle, the occasional weather-beaten road, the river. They called Africa the dark continent, but all Ben could see was a riot of colour.

The landing was a lot less smooth than the one they had experienced in Kinshasa Airport earlier that day – Ben was pleased he had heeded the instruction of the smiling pilot to strap himself in. Finally, though, the vigorously jolting plane came to a stop, the doors were opened and the passengers stepped out into the oppressively humid outside. Ben felt his clothes cling immediately to his skin as Abele pulled down their luggage and carried it to the side of the runway. There was little to distinguish this airfield from any other patch of cracked earth – Ben squinted as he looked around at the unfamiliar, slightly hostile surroundings. Nothing. No buildings, no shelter: just an expanse of earth covered with low brush and brown dust. Abele spoke to the pilot in an African dialect: he shook his head and then walked over to Ben and his father, hand outstretched and grin still intact, revealing several misshapen, yellow teeth interspersed with four or five gaps.

'You are not coming to the village with us?' Ben's dad asked in that loud, slow voice people use when addressing someone who doesn't speak their language.

If anything, the pilot's grin became wider as he shook his head and waved a finger in front of him, before turning and clambering back into the cockpit. The Cessna was gone as quickly as it had arrived, leaving the three of them alone with their bags and an uncomfortable silence, staring as the plane disappeared into the skies.

By the side of the road was a small copse of palm

trees which cast a long shadow in the afternoon sun. The trio took shelter in the shade as Ben and his dad waited for Abele to tell them how they were to be transported from here. 'They send someone to collect us,' he murmured, before turning his back on his two English companions and gazing out into the distance. Ben peered around him. The mid-afternoon sun was causing a wavy haze of heat in the near distance, making it difficult for him to focus on any one thing, even with the expensive Polaroid shades his mum had insisted on buying for him. In one direction, though – a mile away, perhaps less, perhaps more – he saw something moving across the horizon. It was a crowd of animals, travelling at some speed, though he could not make out what they were.

Suddenly he jumped as he heard Abele's voice right next to him. 'Olive baboon,' he noted, a look of distaste in his face.

'Are they dangerous?' Ben asked, unable to take his eyes off the troop.

Abele shrugged. 'Not wise to get too close. But more nuisance than dangerous. They steal food.'

Just then their attention was distracted from the baboons by the quivering, hazy sight of a car appearing in the distance. Abele raised his arm in the air and stood by the side of the road while Ben and his father waited wordlessly behind him. It took the car longer to reach them than Ben would have expected – it was a beaten-up old thing, trundling slowly along. Finally, though, it pulled up at a short distance – perhaps ten metres – from the trio, who were eagerly awaiting its arrival. The driver switched off the noisy engine, opened his door and started walking towards them. The smile on his face was perhaps broader even than that of the pilot who had just left them, though he walked with a curious posture, his hands held firmly behind his back. Noting the presence of two white men, he spoke in broken English. 'You want lift?'

From the corner of his eye, Ben saw Abele's brow furrow, and in that split second he himself realized that what this stranger had just said to them was odd. If he'd been sent to pick them up, why would he be asking them if they wanted a lift? He took an involuntary step backwards, but it was too late. He froze as the man let the smile fall from his face and pulled his hands from behind his back to reveal a dull, grey handgun.

Nobody moved. Ben felt a drop of sweat drip down the right-hand side of his face, though whether that was a result of the heat or the sudden fear that was like a shock through his body, he couldn't tell. He stared at the man who had them at gunpoint. His lip was curled now, and there was a look of flat menace in his eyes that suggested to Ben he would not hesitate to use his weapon if they didn't do exactly what he said – or even if they did.

Their attacker twitched the gun down towards the bags. 'Empty them,' he commanded.

Ben and his father glanced at Abele, who nodded at them. Ben was the first to bend down to his bag. 'Slow!' the attacker barked, the word spoken with such sharp urgency that for a millisecond he thought it was the sound of the gun firing. Struggling to keep control of himself, Ben slowed his movements down, unzipped his luggage and then started to upturn it.

But before he could spill its contents onto the dusty ground, there was movement.

The attacker had stepped closer to Abele who, with a quickness that Ben would never have expected of him, shot out his hand and grabbed the arm with which their attacker was holding the gun. There was a brief struggle, and suddenly the gun went off. The bang rang in Ben's ears and caused a host of unfamiliar birds to rise as one from their hiding places in the low brush. Ben and his father watched in frozen horror as the two men struggled to get control of the weapon. They were an evenly matched pair – both strong, both desperate – but eventually the attacker managed to strike Abele a vicious blow across the side of the face. Abele's head twisted round and he fell with a heavy thud to his knees as the attacker took a couple of steps backwards and aimed the gun directly at Abele's face.

There was a wildness in the man's eyes that put Ben in no doubt that he was about to shoot. He had to do something.

As quick as his trembling limbs would allow him to, he plunged his hand into his bag and grabbed the first hard object he came across – the bottle of water he had promised his mum he would pack. With a yank he pulled it out, ignoring his other belongings, which tumbled out onto the ground, and hurled it at the attacker. The bottle hit him squarely on the side of the face, suddenly distracting him, and for a short moment Ben thought he had done enough.

But he hadn't. For the second time in as many minutes, the gun cracked loudly, reverberating with a horrible quake through Ben's body.

'Abele!' he and his father shouted desperately in unison as their guide started to fall.

It all happened as though in slow motion. Abele lurched forward and in an instant Ben's desperation turned to sudden relief as he realized that their attacker had missed him and that Abele was seizing his moment – and his assailant. He grabbed the man's legs below the knees and the car driver fell to the ground, coughing loudly and hoarsely as he was struck with great fierceness in the pit of his stomach. Momentarily winded, he could do nothing but lie in the dust. Russell ran towards him to retrieve the weapon before he had time to recuperate, but Abele was already there. He banged the man's wrist vigorously against a sharp stone that was on the ground, causing it to bleed immediately and profusely, then grabbed the gun from his outstretched palm. 'Get in the car,' he shouted to them as he stood up, the gun aimed directly at the abdomen of the suddenly terrified attacker.

Ben stuffed his belongings back into his bag, then he and his dad started dragging the luggage towards the vehicle. He was vaguely aware of Abele circling around their assailant in the direction of the car, gun still pointing firmly at him; but when they were just a metre away from the vehicle, Ben looked back over his shoulder to see Abele stepping towards the prostrate man, the gun pointed straight at his head.

He meant to shoot him.

'Abele!' Ben shouted. 'No!' He dropped the bag and ran towards the guide, whose eyes flickered towards him, his face confused.

'Leave them, Ben,' his dad shouted, but Ben ignored him. He was standing next to Abele now, and knew he had to talk quickly.

'You can't just kill him, Abele.'

'This man was going to take my life,' Abele said in an emotionless voice, as though that excused everything.

'I don't care,' Ben told him, his voice low and urgent. 'Just get in the car – we'll leave him here.'

Abele looked back at the man, who was still lying on the floor, dread in his eyes. Ben suddenly became aware that he was muttering something in a strange language under his breath. A prayer, perhaps, though whether it was one of forgiveness or protection, Ben couldn't tell. Abele walked up to him and, after appearing to pause for thought, kicked him hard in the side of the ribs. The man groaned again and doubled up as he lay on the ground. Abele spoke – Ben didn't understand what he said – then repeated himself more harshly. Their attacker painfully got to his feet, raised his arms in the air, and stepped backwards until he was a good distance from them. 'Now get in the car.' Abele repeated his instruction to Ben.

This time, Ben did as he was told. He and his dad heaved their bags into the boot, then Ben took a seat in the back while his dad sat in the front. Abele walked backwards towards the car, still pointing the gun at their assailant, who stared after them with contempt etched on his face. The keys were in the ignition, so as soon as Abele sat in the driving seat and placed the gun on the dashboard, they were away.

As they drove past their attacker, Ben watched him from the back window. His lip was still curled, and his yellow eyes followed Ben, boring intently into his features. There was hate on his face, Ben thought, and humiliation. He tried to look for a sign of thanks – Ben had saved his life, after all – but there was none.

They drove down the road in a silence that was punctuated only by the grumbling of the car as it struggled on the bumpy track. Ben watched his father. His balding head was red and dotted with beads of sweat, but his face seemed pale and gaunt. Now and then he opened his mouth as if to speak, but then thought better of it. In the end, it was Abele who broke the silence for him. Keeping one hand on the steering wheel, he took the gun from the dashboard and carefully handed it to Russell. 'Do you know how to use it?' he asked.

'I really don't think . . .' Russell started to say, but his voice petered out at a withering look from Abele.

'I have already told you,' he intoned, 'my country is a very dangerous place, and you insist on coming to the most dangerous part. We have been fighting each other in civil war for many years, and life is not held in high regard. You never know when you will meet *voleurs* like him – the rule of law is weak here. Take the gun.'

There was a silence before Abele spoke again.

'You might need it,' he said.

CHAPTER FIVE

It took an uncomfortable half-hour to drive to the village of Udok, and in that time they saw nobody else on the road: they were clearly travelling to a place more out of the way than Ben had supposed. As they drove, he observed the vegetation on the side of the roads growing thicker and denser; soon, though, it started to clear as they approached the village.

There was nothing to mark where the no man's land of jungle finished and the village began – there was just the occasional deserted hut, and then a lone villager staring curiously at this strange car passing by. As the surroundings became more populated, Abele drove the car slowly: animals as well as humans, each as scrawny as the other, were wandering in what passed as a road, clearly unused to the presence of motor vehicles. Occasionally a few children would run alongside the car, doing what they could to be high-spirited; but there seemed something rather half-hearted about their game, and they soon melted away.

The centre of the village was a large square, in the middle of which was a covered marketplace. There was room for perhaps fifty stalls there, but Ben could only make out two – one selling cloth, the other selling some kind of gnarled vegetable he could not identify at such a distance. Around the edge of the square were the familiar corrugated-iron huts. Some of them had the appearance of shops – there was a motley collection of goods for sale outside them – but custom seemed to be slow. Indeed, there seemed to be too few people to warrant such a number of outlets; those that Ben could see appeared to be walking hurriedly, keeping themselves to themselves.

There was one exception. Abele stopped the car to let a man cross the street. He walked with crutches, as one leg was missing and the other ended in a cloth-bound stump where the foot used to be. His face was covered in deep white scars and one of his eyes was closed over. 'What happened to him?' Ben whispered.

'Landmine,' Abele replied shortly. 'They are a big problem in my country. Unexploded. He is not the only person you will see in this state. There are many, and not just men – women and children too.'

By the time Abele had finished speaking, the land-mine victim had completed his painful walk across the street, and the car drove on.

Russell coughed. 'These landmines,' he asked. 'Where are they, exactly?'

Abele's face broke into what passed for a smile. 'If we knew where they were, Mr Tracey, you would not be seeing people in that condition.'

'Then the road we just drove up, there could be . . .'

'Yes,' Abele agreed. 'There could be landmines there. But it is most likely to be safe. Cars have been driving up that road for many years now since the landmines were planted. Most of those that were hidden there have already done their killing.'

Abele stopped – somewhat randomly, it seemed to Ben – and with a curt 'Wait here' he climbed out of the car and approached a man sitting under the tattered canopy of what appeared to be a café, an earthenware cup in front of him. He spoke to the man and pointed at the car; the man nodded slowly, as though he understood what Abele was saying to him.

'He, um, he seems to know what he's doing.' Ben's father chose his words carefully. It was the first time he had addressed his son since the incident at the air-field, and Ben could tell from his voice that some of the confidence he had displayed earlier in the day had been knocked out of him.

'He was going to kill that man,' Ben observed pointedly.

'Yes, well . . .' his father blustered slightly, before giving up and speaking quietly. 'You did a good thing there, Ben. I'm proud of you. I, er, didn't really anticipate it being so dangerous here, I'll have to admit. And I feel a little uncomfortable with this gun. I don't want you to think that carrying a weapon like this is the right thing to do. I'll get done what I need to do, and we'll get out of here as soon as possible.' He smiled. 'I feel the Kenyan beaches calling, don't you?'

Ben inclined his head slightly, but he was only half listening, more interested in Abele's conversation with the man at the café table, and hardly noticing the small group of children who had congregated by the car and were looking at these two white men with unveiled curiosity. They failed to disperse as Abele strode back to the car. 'Your lodgings are just here, in a compound off the square.'

'Who was that man?' Ben asked.

'One of the mine managers,' Abele replied shortly.

'You know him?'

Abele shook his head. 'Only the managers have money in this village to buy *malefu* – palm wine,' he explained simply. 'He knew you were expected.'

Ben's father spoke. 'Did, er, did he say why there

was no one at the airfield to pick us up – no one, um, *official*, I mean . . .'

Abele shrugged. 'Maybe the message that you were coming a day earlier did not get through. There is only one satellite telephone in the village, and often the connection is poor. Come, he told me where you will stay – I will show you.'

Carrying their luggage with an ease that still surprised Ben, Abele led them from the car through a rusty metal gate and into a small compound. It consisted of three stone buildings with wooden doors, all set around a central courtyard that housed the debris of daily life in these parts – large metal washing buckets, rusting grills for food, chunks of tree trunks dotted around as seats. But even though the courtyard itself suggested signs of life, there were none: the place was deserted. 'Where *is* everyone?' Ben asked in a slightly awed whisper.

Abele refused to answer. He just carried their things into one of the buildings. 'They're probably all sheltering from the sun,' Ben's dad said, before following Abele in. Ben looked up at the sky. The sun was low now – it would be setting soon – and the heat had begun to dissipate. If people were staying in their houses, that wasn't the reason.

He followed them into the building. Inside it was very simple. There were two beds – each little more than a mattress on a square concrete block with a mosquito net hanging from the ceiling. A rickety table with two chairs was the only other furnishing. At the back of the room was a door leading to an outdoor toilet, covered only by a sheet of the seemingly omnipresent corrugated iron. Abele dumped the luggage on the floor, then turned to Ben's dad. 'You should stay in here,' he told him. 'I will bring you food later.' He walked out without another word, closing the thin wooden door behind him.

It was dark in the hut, the only light coming from the small window, which was covered by a thick mosquito net. Ben's father placed the gun on the table with a certain amount of relief that he no longer had to carry it, then lay down on his bed. 'I think I'd like to get some rest,' he told his son, and within minutes he was asleep.

Ben, however, had other things on his mind. He knew Abele's concern for their welfare stemmed as much from his superstitions – whatever they were – as from the fact that this was a volatile place, so surely he could not expect dangerous encounters like the one they had just experienced to occur in the middle of the village.

Besides, he had a promise to keep.

From his bag he pulled a small cotton rucksack; then, for safe measure, he turned his attention to the gun. It was heavier than he expected, and on the side was a small grey safety catch, still in the off position. For a moment he shuddered to think that it could have gone off in his dad's hand at any moment; but with a gentle click he switched it on, then placed the gun in his bag, zipped it up and crept out of the room and through the gate of the compound.

The car had been driven away, though not by Abele, who was to be seen disappearing round a corner. Ben shrugged it off and looked around him. The central square was still almost deserted, but there were a few villagers going about their business. Ben approached one of them – an old man wearing a multicoloured but faded tunic. 'Excuse me!' he called, and the man stopped. He looked at Ben suspiciously, and took a faltering step backwards when he came too close. 'I'm looking for someone,' Ben said clearly and with what he hoped was a reassuring smile on his face.

The man shook his head, obviously not under-standing what Ben was saying, so he tried again, this time in the best French he could muster. '*Je cherche quelqu'un . . .*'

This time the man nodded, but the mistrust did not leave his eyes.

'Halima.' Ben spoke the name the cleaning lady had uttered.

In an instant, the man put his head down and walked away as though Ben had not even been there.

Ben made to follow him, but stopped himself. What had he said to this man? Why had he ignored him in that way? He looked around to find someone else he could ask; this time he selected a large woman with intricately plaited hair. But the response was the same – a hasty mutter and suddenly she was gone.

Then Ben remembered the children – as they had entered the village, they had seemed less wary of the strangers. He scanned around until he saw a single child – perhaps eight years old – sitting by himself under the branches of a tree, drawing in the dust with a twig. The boy only had one arm – another landmine casualty, Ben surmised. He approached him and with a smile said the word 'Halima?'

The little boy looked up at him. His dark brown eyes seemed unusually large on his face, and he had a serious expression. He nodded his head.

'Can you take me to her?' Ben asked, reinforcing his question by pointing at himself then making a walking movement with his fingers.

The little boy nodded again, stood up, and led the way.

The house to which he took Ben was located off the central square, down a winding little street that led to another clearing. The street itself was deserted, and as he walked down in silence, Ben noticed that some of the houses had an X marked on the door in what looked like red paint. He wanted to ask the boy what it meant, but knew that he would not be able to make himself understood.

Eventually the boy stopped and pointed at one of the doors, before silently turning and walking back up the street. Ben called a word of thanks after him, but it seemed to go unheard.

Suddenly he felt a sense of deep unease, alone in this strange place, not knowing who he was likely to find behind the door of this house. And whatever the marking on the door meant, he felt sure it was unlikely to announce good news. But he had come here to do something, so he took a deep breath and knocked three times on the door.

For a moment there was no answer, so he tried again. This time he heard a rustling from inside, and the door creaked gently open a few centimetres.

Behind the door it was dark, but there was enough light just to make out the features of the girl who had opened it. She was a teenager, just – about fourteen – with large, unblinking eyes and smooth, shiny skin. Her long frizzy hair was pulled back over her scalp, and her pretty face could not hide its surprise at seeing a white boy at her door.

'Halima?' Ben asked softly.

She nodded her head, but said nothing.

'Do you speak any English?'

'Yes.' Her voice was clear, and sounded more confident than her features suggested.

'I have something for you. From your sister.'

Her face creased into a perplexed frown, and Ben noticed how her nose crumpled slightly as she did so. He put his hand in his pocket and pulled out the note and the wooden token. 'From Fatima,' he insisted, and he handed them to Halima. The girl took the gift, gave the note a cursory glance, and then directed her attention to the token. When she saw what was etched on it, her eyes filled with tears and she bit her lip.

'Fatima gave you this?' she asked uncertainly.

Ben nodded his head. 'Um, can I come in?'

Halima looked nervously behind her, then shook her head. 'It would not be right,' she said mysteriously. 'I will walk with you.'

She stepped outside and closed the door behind her. 'When did you see my sister?' she asked as they started walking side by side down the street.

'This morning,' Ben told her.

'She was well?' Halima's gaze seemed to be fixed firmly on the ground as she walked, and she asked the question as though she knew what the answer would be.

'She seemed worried,' Ben admitted. 'She said she had not heard from you or your parents.'

Halima stopped still. 'She mentioned our parents?'

Ben nodded as Halima's eyes gazed back up at him, filling with tears once again.

'She does not know?'

'Know what?'

'I sent her a letter. She did not receive it?'

Ben shook his head. 'She says she has not heard anything from you for months. She's been sending you money, but doesn't think you've been receiving it.'

Halima turned her head away and continued walking. 'My parents died four weeks ago.' She resolutely avoided looking at Ben as she spoke.

They walked in silence for a few moments as Ben struggled to think what to say. 'I'm sorry,' was all he could finally manage.

They had crossed the clearing, and now stood at what appeared to Ben to be the edge of the village. There was a large field ahead of them, and it seemed to his untrained eye that it would once have been forest, as it was covered in the sawn-off stumps of the rubber trees he had seen on his way here. It was a sad sight. Beyond it was thick forest.

'What did they die of?' Ben broke the melancholy silence that had descended on them both.

'They say it was malaria,' Halima stated flatly.

'You don't sound so sure.'

Halima shrugged, and fiddled with the token her sister had sent. 'It's possible,' she whispered. 'Malaria is very bad in these parts.'

'Can I do anything to help?' Ben offered.

Halima smiled – the first time she had done so since they met, and the smile lit up her face. 'You are kind,' she said. 'That is not always a good thing here. But if you want to help, you could start by telling me your name.'

Ben grinned at her. 'Ben Tracey. Pleased to meet you.'

'Welcome to Udok, Ben Tracey.' Halima almost fluttered her eyelashes at him. 'You should know that my fellow villagers will think you are insane if they see you having anything to do with me.' She spoke with a smile, but it was clear that she was quite serious. 'So what is it that brings you here?'

'The mine,' Ben explained shortly. 'My father is a scientist. They want him to do some tests there. I just came along for the ride.'

Halima didn't take her eyes off him. 'The mine.' She repeated his words unenthusiastically.

Ben shot her a questioning glance, but she did not seem to want to elaborate, so he tried a different tack. 'Why is everyone so scared of this village?'

The question seemed to catch Halima off guard. 'What do you mean?' she asked, her eyes suddenly darting around as though she was scared someone would overhear them.

'Everyone is reluctant to come here. And even the villagers I've seen don't seem to want to talk to anyone. Except you.'

Halima brushed his hand with her fingers, and opened her mouth to speak; but before she was able to, Ben heard a man's voice a little distance behind him. 'Ben Tracey?'

Halima looked over his shoulder and her expression turned instantly to one of worry. 'I have to go,' she whispered, and without another word she hurried back across the clearing and up the street in which she lived. Perplexed, Ben turned to see a tall, lanky black man with a shaved head and a prominent, protruding Adam's apple bearing down on him. His brow was furrowed, his face serious; it was only once he was a few metres away that he made the effort to fix his mouth into a more friendly expression.

Ben eyed him warily.

'You should not be wandering about by yourself.' The man's voice was hoarse, like a forced whisper. 'I understand you have already discovered what a dangerous place the Congo can be.'

'I wasn't by myself,' Ben stated boldly. There was something about this man's demeanour that he didn't like.

The man glanced after Halima, but she had already disappeared. When he turned back to Ben, his face had softened slightly. 'Your father was worried,' he rasped. 'He says you have a gun.'

Ben remained stony-faced.

'Give it to me,' the man insisted.

Ben shook his head. There was no way he was going to be left alone in the presence of a strange Congolese man with an automatic handgun – not after what had happened earlier. 'I'll go back to the compound,' he countered abruptly, 'but the gun stays with me.'

The man nodded slowly, as though deciding how to react to Ben's sudden determination. 'Whatever you say, Mr Ben,' he whispered, and the two of them stared directly into each other's eyes. There was no friendship in that stare.

'You go first,' Ben instructed.

The man turned and led the way.

CHAPTER SIX

They walked in silence. Occasionally the man would look back at Ben, his strange yellow eyes peering suspiciously out of his face; Ben stared straight ahead, avoiding the gaze of this man who made him feel so uncomfortable.

Before long they were back at the compound. Ben's dad was in the central yard, his tired face a thunderstorm. 'What on earth do you think you were doing?' he demanded of his son the moment he saw him.

Ben stood squarely in front of his father, fully prepared to defend himself and his actions; but suddenly he felt something on his shoulder. He looked up to see the man who had escorted him home, gently resting his arm on Ben's T-shirt and smiling toothily at his father. 'Do not be too harsh on him,

Mr Tracey,' he said. 'He is right to take precautions.'

Russell Tracey opened his mouth as though to continue the reprimand, but then seemed suddenly to think better of it. 'I think you should go inside, Ben.' He turned to their guest. 'Half past seven tomorrow morning, then, Suliman,' he said politely. The black man nodded, removed his hand from Ben's shoulder, then turned and left.

Once inside, Ben braced himself for the full force of his dad's displeasure, but it didn't come. 'Guns aren't toys, Ben,' was all he saw fit to say – a bit unnecessarily, Ben thought, given the events of the day.

Ben slept fitfully. The food Abele had brought them had been unrecognizable and not to their Western taste – a bowl of thick mashed cassava root, pungently flavoured with unfamiliar herbs. There hadn't been much of it either, and both Ben and his father had gone to bed feeling hungry. The African night was pitch black and unbearably hot and humid – Ben found himself lying under a rough sheet made damp by his own sweat – and despite the fact that the thin mesh of the mosquito net was draped over his bed, his skin felt itchy, as though it were being feasted on by a million unseen insects. And then there were the noises – slithers and rustles and bumps. After a while it became impossible to determine whether they originated from a distance or nearby, or even from inside the hut. Ben had no love of snakes, and by the darkness of midnight, he had imagined all manner of reptilian horrors making their way across the floor of his bedroom.

By the time morning came, his head felt stuffy and his eyes were tight with tiredness, but he was glad to see the steely grey of dawn lighten up the room little by little. He examined his skin for the telltale red welts of the insect bites that he suspected he would be covered with, but the mosquito net appeared to have done its job. Nevertheless, he gratefully gulped down that morning's dose of Lariam, the anti-malaria medication he had been prescribed. As he did so, he remembered with a grim smile the warning the doctor had given him: that the medicine could have certain side effects – dizziness, nausea, even paranoia. He wondered if the uncomfortable feeling he had about this place was down to the drugs. Somehow he didn't think so.

His dad had explained over supper the previous night that today he would be going to the mine with Suliman, the mine manager. Ben was to stay in the village, where Abele would look after him. Ben hadn't argued – the mine didn't hold much interest for him, and he had too many unanswered questions about what was going on round here to be diverted by his dad's dry experiments and sample-taking.

At seven-thirty exactly, Suliman arrived in an old

Land Rover. Flanked by two men who said nothing and lurked at the entrance to the compound, he approached Ben's dad with an outstretched hand and flashed a smile at Ben himself. Any hint of the suspicion he had demonstrated towards Ben the previous day seemed to have disappeared, although he did not seem to want to catch his eye more often than necessary. 'We need to get started, Mr Tracey,' he rasped at Russell. 'There is a lot to get through.'

Russell nodded, then walked over to give Ben a kiss. Ben knew the signs and offered him his hand instead, which his dad shook a little awkwardly. 'Abele should be here soon,' Russell said. 'I'll be back as quickly as I can.'

Ben watched from the entrance to the compound as Suliman ushered his dad into the waiting jeep. It made a deep, throttling sound as it started off, then disappeared, leaving a cloud of dust and an imprint of the tyres in its wake. Ben waited for it to go out of sight, then stood there for a little longer watching the business of the villagers milling about the square. There were more of them this morning than there had been the previous night, but they still walked with that abrupt haste, none of them stopping to speak to their neighbours. It was half an hour before Abele arrived, a loaf of bread in his hands. They greeted each other wordlessly before walking into the compound and sitting down to share the bread in rough hunks. It was hard and tasteless, but Ben was hungry.

'We should stay here today.' Abele broke his silence once he had finished eating.

Ben shook his head. 'Why?'

Abele put his hand out, palm facing upwards. 'The air is thick,' he explained. 'There will be rain soon, and heavy.'

'So what? The worst that can happen is we'll get wet.' Ben smiled as he thought back to the events in London only a few months previously. 'It's only a bit of water.'

Abele looked at him severely. 'When it rains, it will be fierce. You will need to find shelter.'

'All right, all right,' Ben told him a bit indulgently. 'I won't go far, and if it rains I'll come straight back. But I'm definitely going out – you stay here if you want to.'

Abele settled himself more comfortably on his sawn-off tree trunk to indicate that that was precisely what he intended to do. Ben shrugged, rubbed the crumbs off his lap, and wandered out into the main square.

Remembering the advice he had read on the Internet, the first thing he wanted to do was buy drinking water; it would be foolish to assume that his system would easily assimilate the local water like the villagers themselves. He looked around to try and find someone he could ask, but everyone seemed to be avoiding his gaze; if he did catch anyone looking at him, they would jerk their heads down to the ground almost immediately. After a minute or two, a couple of young children came running towards him, shouting words he could not understand; he tried to ask them in slow, simple English where he could buy bottles of water, but they clearly did not know what he was talking about and carried on shouting at him.

But then, from the corner of his eye, he saw a figure he recognized at the other side of the square. It was Halima, dressed identically to the way she had been the previous day. Trying to ignore the children clutching at his legs, he waved at her, his right arm forming a large arc in the air. Halima appeared not to notice him, keeping her eyes resolutely in front of her, so to attract her attention he shouted her name. 'Halima!' he called. 'Over here!'

As soon as he did so, Ben felt self-conscious. Everyone in the square turned momentarily to look at him before going back to what they were doing. Halima did the same, but unlike all the others she kept her eyes on him a little longer. Her face scrunched up into what looked to Ben like a gesture of warning, and she shook her head sharply before turning and walking out of the square.

Ben watched her leave, perplexed by her actions. She had seemed so eager to speak to him yesterday – what had caused her to walk away like that now? Still trying to work this out, he strode purposefully away from the children at his feet, a frown on his face, keeping a lookout for somewhere he could buy water.

On the other side of the square there was a hut with a few old red crates outside. Ben approached to see that they held unmarked bottles with silvery metal lids. Most of them contained what looked like water; a few seemed to be filled with cola, others with a milky liquid he couldn't identify. He helped himself to two bottles of water, then walked inside, pulling a note out of his pocket as he did so.

It took his eyes a few moments to get used to the darkness inside. When he did so, he saw an old woman, her skin dry and wrinkled, staring un-smilingly at him. She sat on a high wooden stool, surrounded by other bottle crates, though these were uniformly empty. Ben held up the bottles to indicate that he wanted to buy them, then thrust the note towards her. Her hand lashed out more quickly than her frailty would have suggested it could, and she stuffed it into a pouch tied round her waist, pulling out a few coins change and handing them to Ben in return. As she did so, however, there was a sudden commotion at the door. Ben spun round to see another woman standing in the doorway, a water bottle in her hand. The shopkeeper spat some harsh words at her in Lingala, which the woman responded to equally harshly, and a loud argument followed, with Ben standing somewhat perplexed in the middle of it. The shopkeeper jumped from her stool with surprising agility and snatched the bottle back from her surprised customer, the two of them shouting at each other all the while.

Amidst all the confusion, Ben heard a voice. It was Abele, standing just outside the hut, calling to Ben to come out. Skirting round the edge of the ongoing argument, he slipped outside. 'Blimey.' He smiled at Abele. 'What was all that about?'

Abele's face remained severe. 'The woman owes the shopkeeper money. She wants to take more water, but the shopkeeper will not let her until she pays her bills. The woman is saying that her husband is very sick. He needs clean water or he will die.'

Ben listened in horror to what Abele was saying. 'You mean they can't get clean water without paying for it?'

Abele shrugged. 'There is a tap in the village, but the water there is not always the cleanest.' As he spoke, the woman stormed out of the shop, past the two of them, and off towards the centre of the square. Ben ran after her. 'Excuse me!' he shouted. The woman turned, the surprise of seeing this young white boy calling her evident in her face. As he approached, Ben held out one of the bottles of water he had bought. 'Take it,' he said, thrusting it into her hands.

The woman looked at the bottle, then back at Ben. There was a wariness in her eyes, but she did not refuse the gift, simply nodding her head in a curt gesture of appreciation. Then she turned and walked quickly away.

Ben watched her go. Gradually he became aware of Abele standing just behind him. 'You will not be able to give charity to everyone who is sick in this village, Ben,' he murmured.

Ben didn't take his eyes off the woman. 'I thought you said you were going to stay in the compound, Abele,' he retorted, beginning to feel a bit irritated by his constant cryptic comments.

Abele remained stony-faced. 'I am here to look after you,' he said shortly.

'Come on, then.' The woman was turning round a corner, so Ben ran after her with Abele running reluctantly behind. He was beginning to have a suspicion, and he wanted to see if he was right.

Sure enough, as he turned the corner, he saw the

woman opening the wooden door to a shabby-looking hut. Looking over her shoulder, she saw Ben, but she quickly pulled her gaze away, stepped inside and slammed the door shut. Ben approached. Painted on the door in thick red paint – just as it had been at Halima's house – there was a cross. 'That's what it means, isn't it?' Ben asked breathlessly. 'They paint a red cross when someone is dying in the house.'

'Or *has* died,' Abele noted darkly.

Ben walked away from the house, checking the doors of the other huts in this ramshackle street. Red crosses adorned the fronts of almost half of them. 'What's wrong with all these people?' he breathed, his head suddenly spinning at the thought of so much death. He turned to Abele.

His face made it clear he had nothing to say on the subject; he just fingered the charm that hung around his neck.

Suliman had not accompanied Russell into the deepest part of the mine; it had not been necessary. As mine manager he had to attend to the workers excavating for tin elsewhere, so he had left the scientist in the hands of one of his colleagues, a rather surly villager who spoke no English but seemed very nervous as he held a torch to the exposed rock face positioned just by the underground lake from which

Russell was taking his samples. It was hard work and Russell was soon damp with sweat despite the fact that it was cool in the caves. He would have liked to splash water from the lake over his face, but he knew how foolish that would be: cholera, tapeworms – it could be hiding all manner of parasites and diseases.

It was unusual to find Coltan down here. It was normally surface-mined, but there had been instances of it being discovered as an offshoot of other mining operations. And of course it would take him a while to do all the proper tests at his lab back in the UK, but he could already tell that this was a rich source of the good stuff, and he would be able to give his findings to Kruger and the others back in Kinshasa. That would please them, and at least he would feel as if one part of his excursion into Africa with Ben had gone the way it should. Russell had to admit that things hadn't really been going according to plan. If Ben seemed jumpy around everyone, it wasn't really much of a surprise. He was only a young boy, after all, and all things considered, his father thought he was coping quite well. If only he hadn't seemed so openly suspicious of Kruger and Suliman, two men who seemed to be doing their very best to make everything run smoothly.

Ah well, Russell thought to himself. That sort of maturity will come. In time.

He glanced at his watch in the torchlight. It was getting on, so he turned and nodded to his companion with a smile. 'We'll finish now,' he said in loud, overly pronounced tones that he knew the guy wouldn't understand, but he hoped he would get his drift.

The man nodded and turned round, eager to leave. 'I still need the light here!' Russell called, spinning round and grabbing him by the arm. The man uttered some harsh words in a deep voice, pulling his arm away from Russell, his face sinister and demonic by the light of the torch. As he lowered the torch, something caught Russell's eye. 'Shine it there,' he instructed, pointing out over the water. His companion did as he was told. A small animal – a bat, most likely, Russell thought – was flailing in the water, struggling.

And then, quite suddenly, it fell silent.

Its death seemed to bring an increased chill into the cave. Russell dragged his attention away and packed up his things, and the two of them started walking along the rickety wooden flooring that would eventually lead them out of the mine. They trudged along in silence, the black man holding the torch, Russell keeping his eyes firmly on the potentially treacherous ground.

As they were leaving the cave, he saw another dead bat, right in front of him, its body already decaying.

He said nothing, but his scientist's brain started ticking over. Clearly there was a colony down here somewhere, a great many of them, no doubt. With such a large population, the probability of seeing dead individuals was high. He smiled to himself. There was something satisfying about seeing statistics in action.

Had he directed the beam back across the water, however, Russell might have noticed a small opening into an adjoining cave. He could never have reached it to explore, even if he had wanted to, because the only way of accessing it was across the water. Had he been able to, however, he would have been horrified by what he saw on the banks of the underground lake.

Thousands upon thousands of bats.

All of them dead.

All of them piled high in a mountain of increasingly rotten and stinking flesh.

Ben's dad returned to the compound later that afternoon. Abele had insisted that he and Ben should go back, and Ben's recent discovery that half the huts in the village seemed to be housing the sick and dying had dampened his enthusiasm for exploring, so he had sought shelter from the heat and the increasingly intolerable humidity by lying on his bed in the half darkness. Now, though, it was beginning to cool down.

Russell looked grimy and tired – more tired than

Ben had seen him in a long time in fact, with large, black rings under his eyes and a faintly haggard expression. He entered the compound with Suliman sticking close to him. Both men had sweat on their bald heads, though Suliman looked more comfortable with it than Russell.

'Good day?' Ben asked his dad.

Russell nodded. 'It's a rich source of good-quality Coltan. I need another day there, and then we can get back.' He turned to Suliman. 'Thank you for your kindness today,' he said politely. 'Same time tomorrow?'

'My people will be here to collect you.' Suliman bowed slightly, and made to leave.

'Just a minute!' Ben said sharply. 'I want to ask you a question.'

Suliman turned, and Ben felt both men's eyes on him.

'What's making everyone so ill? Why is everyone dying?'

'Ben!' Russell reprimanded. 'I don't want to hear you speaking to our hosts so rudely.'

'It's true, Dad. Every other house in this village has a red cross painted on the door. It means that some-one is dying, or has died recently, in that house. We've been brought here without being told – I think we deserve to know what's going on.'

Suliman looked intently at him, his face hard before it suddenly dissolved into a softer smile. 'It's true, Ben,' he whispered, his rasping voice sounding almost snakelike. 'Many of our villagers are sick. You are taking your malaria medication, I hope?'

Ben nodded mutely.

'Good. It has been bad lately. A very vicious strain. The dead are as numerous as those who survive it. Few people can afford the medicine.'

Ben said nothing; malaria was a big problem in the area, that much he knew, and Suliman's explanation had the desperate ring of truth.

'Our people have no option but to accept this as a way of life,' Suliman continued. Then he nodded at Ben and his father in turn. 'Until tomorrow, then,' he said, and left.

There was a silence between Ben and his father, which Russell broke in his quiet voice. 'Now do you understand why I was so insistent that you took your malaria medication before we left?' he asked in that frustratingly smug voice Ben found adults often using with him.

'I suppose so,' Ben muttered. He knew he was being surly, but he couldn't help it. He was beginning to wish he had never come.

CHAPTER SEVEN

Russell Tracey's breathing was heavy, slow and measured. Ben hadn't noticed it the previous night – probably too busy worrying about creepy crawlies in the bedroom, he supposed. He lay drowsily in the darkness listening to it, wishing that he too could be visited by the sleep that had descended on his father.

Gradually, though, he became aware of another sound – a scratching in the courtyard outside. He concentrated on isolating that sound from any others and realized that it was footsteps walking across the dusty, gritty earth. And then he heard a tapping at the door. Three gentle knocks. A pause, and they came again – *tap*, *tap*, *tap* – a little louder this time. Russell's breathing remained heavy – clearly he had been undisturbed by the sound – so Ben climbed out from under his mosquito net and pulled on his clothes. He stepped towards the door before halting, turning back on himself and removing the gun from its place on the table. Then he walked to the door and, his finger nervously caressing the trigger of the gun, gently nudged it open.

The African night was sultry, and for a moment Ben thought he had been hearing things as there appeared to be nobody there. He noticed that he was suddenly breathing as heavily as his father, and he prepared to close the door and get back to the relative comfort of his bed when he saw a figure appearing from the shadows. Whoever it was was walking swiftly towards him and had their finger pressed firmly against their lips. Ben felt a sudden sickness of panic rising in his chest, and he felt his arm bringing the gun up to point in front of him.

It wasn't until the figure was almost upon him that he realized who it was.

Halima stopped in her tracks when she saw the gun pointing towards her, her wide eyes staring fearfully at Ben, who immediately let the weapon drop to his side. 'What are you doing?' he whispered at her.

'Come with me,' Halima breathed.

'Where?'

'I need to show you something.'

Ben thought for a moment. His dad would be

furious if he sneaked off again, especially with the gun. But he was asleep, and showed no signs of waking up soon, so Ben decided on a compromise. 'Wait there,' he told Halima, before slipping back inside, placing the weapon in its place on the table, and then returning to see what this mysterious girl wanted with him.

'Come with me,' Halima repeated, and she led him out into the main square.

There was nobody about, but the square itself was almost eerily well-lit by the bright silver light of the waxing moon. 'We need to stay hidden,' Halima told Ben as they skirted quietly round the edge of the square towards the little street where her house was.

'Why?' Ben asked. 'What are we doing? Why did you ignore me earlier on today?' He had so many questions.

'I will explain everything when we get there.' Halima smiled at him a bit apologetically. Suddenly she raised her hand and gestured at him to stop. 'Listen,' she instructed.

Ben stood perfectly still. Somewhere, not too far away, he imagined, he could hear the faint sound of a drum. It played a simple rhythm – three short strokes followed by four quicker ones.

Dum, dum, dum, da-da-da-da.

Halima nodded to herself in approval, then

gestured at Ben to follow her. They sneaked down the street, past Halima's house and on towards the clearing where they had been chatting before Suliman had interrupted them. As they moved, the sound of the drumming grew louder, and it seemed to Ben that it had grown a little faster too. Soon enough, they came to the clearing. On the other side of it, obscured by the thicket of dense trees and brush, Ben could make out the glow of a fire. He felt a tingle of apprehension run down his spine as he realized how foolhardy he was being, allowing this girl he barely knew to lead him around surreptitiously like this in the middle of the night. He stretched out and grabbed her lightly by the arm.

'Halima, I'm not going any further until you tell me what this is about.'

Halima looked down at his hand, but Ben did not move it away. 'We can't stay here out in the open,' she told him seriously. 'I am taking you to see a tribal ritual. The village elders would be very angry if they knew I was showing it to a white person. Some things are not allowed.'

Dum, dum, dum, da-da-da-da. The drumming was closer.

Ben nodded. Halima scurried away to the left, with Ben following. Down the side of the clearing was a pathway with a few trees and straggly bushes providing a little camouflage. It wasn't much, but it was something, and they ran as light-footedly as they could towards the foliage, the light and the sound of the drums.

Once they were in the thicket, they could move with less fear of being seen, but Ben soon found that he had to tread more carefully; the sound of dried wood breaking under his feet made his heart stop every time it happened – he was thankful that the drumming, almost frenzied now, was loud enough to disguise what he felt was his terrible clumsiness.

Dum, dum, dum, da-da-da-da.

They came to the edge of small clearing, and Halima stopped, gently resting her hand on Ben's arm to indicate that he should do the same. In the middle of the clearing was a fire – clearly the one that they had seen from a distance – and sitting around it, about twenty metres from where Ben and Halima were hiding, were eight or nine elderly men. They wore simple clothes – dark-coloured all-in-one tunics mostly – but round their necks they wore what looked like heavy ceramic jewellery. Two of them wore headdresses made from the fur of animals. Standing a little way apart from these men was the drummer, bent double over a large wooden *djembe* drum, intently beating out the increasingly wild rhythm.

Dum, dum, dum, da-da-da-da.

The eyes of all the men were trained on a figure Ben could not see clearly. It was positioned on the other side of the fire, so all he could make out was a silhouette of what appeared to be a man, fairly tall and, as far as Ben could make out, naked, at least from the waist up. He was dancing in time to the rhythm of the drum, not in a wild, frenetic way, but making short, jerky movements.

Ben found himself transfixed by the sinister sight. How long he watched before Halima interrupted his trance he could not have said. 'It is a dance for the ancestors,' she told him.

Ben blinked and turned to look at her. 'What?'

'A dance for the ancestors. The man you see dancing has great power.'

'I don't understand,' Ben whispered. 'Who are the ancestors?'

Halima gazed into the middle distance. 'The dead. Those that have gone before us. It is our duty to ensure that they should not be disturbed.'

'What do you mean, disturbed? How can you disturb dead people?'

Halima gave him a sidelong glance. 'You asked me before why everyone seemed so scared of this village.'

Ben nodded. 'I think I'm already beginning to understand,' he said. 'I know what the red crosses on the doors mean. I know that lots of people are dying here.'

'But do you know why?'

'Suliman told me it was malaria. We were warned about it before we left England.'

Halima smiled faintly. 'Malaria.' She nodded. 'Yes. That is what everyone in the village will tell you. But it is not what they believe.'

'But you told me yourself that your parents died from malaria.'

Ben was puzzled, and Halima clearly understood that from the look on his face. 'You have to understand,' she told him quietly, 'that things are not always what they seem to be in Africa. You are a stranger, so people will not always tell you what they really believe.' She was looking at him intently now. 'I have seen many people die, and I nursed my parents to their graves. What killed them was not malaria. Similar, maybe. But not malaria.'

'Then what was it?'

Halima gazed towards the fire once more. 'My father worked in the mine,' she told him. 'When the mine-owners came, people were worried. They wanted to dig near the burial grounds sacred to our ancestors. But there was nobody to stop them, and besides, they offered jobs and money. We are very poor here, and the village elders welcomed them. To start with there was no problem. But not long ago they extended their excavations, and that was when the mine-workers started to fall ill.'

'All of them?' Ben asked, his attention rapt.

Halima shook her head. 'No. Not all of them. My father and two others first. Then my mother.' Her voice was expressionless as she explained what had happened. 'He woke up one morning vomiting and unable to stand up. His head ached so badly that he could barely speak, he was hot all over and I could hear the breath rattling in his chest. He could eat nothing. My mother became ill the following day. They both died on the same night, eight days after my father fell ill.'

'I'm sorry,' Ben breathed, his expression of sympathy seeming desperately inadequate.

'At first I too believed it was malaria. Even after they died I was not sure I wanted to believe what is so obvious to me now. But it cannot be ignored. Two thirds of the men who have gone down the mine have succumbed to the same illness. Of those people, three quarters have died. In addition, certain members of the mine-workers' families have started to succumb. Everyone in the village knows somebody who has died.'

Ben felt a trickle of sweat drip down the side of his face. The night was warm enough as it was, but the fire was sufficiently large for him to feel it against his skin, despite the fact that they were perhaps twenty metres from it. 'Why have you brought me all the way here to tell me this?' he asked, his voice cracking.

Halima nodded towards the scene in front of them. 'What you are watching is a ceremony to appease the ancestors.' She smiled at him again, and Ben noticed for the first time the orange of the fire reflected in her dark eyes. 'You haven't asked me yet how it is that I speak English.'

This was true – it was something that Ben had wondered, but he hadn't yet had the opportunity to ask.

'I have a radio in my house,' Halima explained, 'one that I listen to as often as possible. There is much to be learned from your World Service.'

Ben remained silent – it wasn't something he had ever listened to.

'So I know something about your culture. No doubt you think that these ideas are stupid. I brought you here to show you how deeply my people believe in them. And to urge you, if you value your life, to leave this place as soon as possible. It is cursed.'

C'est maudit. It was not the first time somebody had told him this.

Ben looked fearfully back at the ceremony. There was no denying that these people certainly looked as if they were taking it extremely seriously. The beating of the drum was more frenzied than ever now, and the village elders seemed to be in a trance-like state of intense concentration. All eyes were fixed on the jerking movements of the silhouetted dancer. Ben suppressed a shudder – here in the darkness of the African night, what Halima was telling him seemed far from improbable. 'So the man dancing,' he whispered, 'is he a—?'

'Yes,' Halima interrupted. 'He is what you would call a witch doctor, but it is not a word we would use. To us he is a healer, and tonight he is trying to heal the rift that exists between the villagers and the ancestors.'

As she spoke, and as though drawn to them by his discussion, the dancer traced the course of a semicircle round the fire. As he came into the light, Ben became aware of his own breath, heavy and trembling. The healer was tall and bony, his skin bare apart from a short cloth skirt. Round his neck he wore colourful beads, and the top of his head was covered by an intricate headdress made of feathers and other things that Ben could not make out.

But it was not his attire that commanded attention; it was his face.

The skin was impossibly wrinkled, so much so that it barely seemed human. Occasionally he would open his mouth into a sinister rictus grin; even from a distance Ben could see that his teeth, such as they were, were bent and decayed. It was the eyes, though, that Ben knew he would never forget. They rolled in their sockets like marbles spinning across the floor; they were yellow and bloodshot.

And then, suddenly, they were looking directly at him.

He shouted a harsh, monosyllabic word and immediately the drumming stopped. The healer raised his arm and pointed precisely in the direction of where Ben and Halima were hiding; as he did so, Ben heard his companion gasp, and then forcefully whisper a single word: 'Run!'

The two of them turned and sprinted their way back through the thicket, all pretence of secrecy obliterated by their blind panic. As he ran, Ben felt a sharp branch whip across one side of his face; it stung, and there was the telltale feeling of moistness on his cheek that told him he had been cut, but he couldn't let it slow him down any more than he could risk looking behind to see if he was being chased. Halima ran by his side – they were well matched in terms of speed – and soon they found themselves at the tree-lined pathway down which they had sneaked only ten minutes before. Now they hurtled up it like their lives depended on it. Ben didn't even fully know what he was running from; he only knew that it was the right thing to do.

As they neared the other end of the pathway, Ben allowed himself a quick glance over his shoulder. There appeared to be no one behind them, although it was difficult to be sure in the darkness, and he felt the tension that had been spurring him on dissipate a little. He turned his head back round to the front and then, along with Halima, came to a sudden, abrupt halt.

Because there, standing in front of them, his arms crossed and his face unreadable, was Suliman.

The two friends stood, wide-eyed and out of breath, in front of him. He looked first at Halima, and then at Ben. 'It is very late for you to be out, Ben,' he rasped.

Ben said nothing as he held his head high, doing his best to exude a confidence he did not feel.

'I think it is time for you to return to your compound,' Suliman insisted. Then he turned his attention to Halima, saying something abruptly to her in Kikongo, and gesturing that she should come with him. Halima shook her head and took a step backwards. Suliman made as if to approach her, but he was blocked by Ben, who had moved between him and his new friend.

'I'll take her home,' he said.

Suliman's gaze remained level as he considered his response. Finally he smiled – an unpleasant smile – and stepped out of his way. 'I think that would be a very good idea,' he replied, before barking something again at Halima. She lowered her eyes to the ground; as she did so, Ben took her hand and led her away.

They wanted to run, but something forced them both to walk briskly and in silence, feeling Suliman's eyes burn into their backs as they went. It was not until minutes later when they found themselves in Halima's street that Ben allowed himself to look back. There was nobody in sight.

'Are you OK?' he asked.

Halima nodded.

'What did he say to you? Before we left, I mean.'

'He said,' Halima replied slowly, 'that he would deal with me in the morning.'

Ben felt his lips tighten. 'You can come and stay with us if you want.'

Halima shook her head. 'No. I don't believe he will disturb me tonight.' She looked back over her shoulder. 'That man has never liked me. They made him mine manager only recently, after the previous one died. Before that he was nobody. No one can understand why they put him in charge.' She made a brave attempt to smile. 'I can lock my door from the inside,' she assured him. 'I'll see you tomorrow, Ben Tracey.'

She turned to open the door. 'Wait!' Ben interrupted her. What she had just said about Suliman had crystallized a question in his mind.

Halima threw him a quizzical glance.

'There's something I don't understand. If the mine is cursed, why don't all the mine-workers die?'

The girl raised one eyebrow. As she did so, she unbuttoned the top of the colourful blouse she was wearing and pulled out a necklace. She held it up to Ben. It bore two tokens: the one that Fatima had sent, and another – smaller but with the same design. 'I am not the only one who has asked for protection,' she whispered. And with that, she opened the door and slipped inside.

Ben waited until he heard the click of the lock before walking quickly and nervously back to his own bed.

CHAPTER EIGHT

Ben's head spun for what seemed like hours, and he lay there turning the events of the evening over in his mind and listening to his father's heavy breathing; but sometime before morning, sleep overcame him.

He was awakened by a bump. Bleary-eyed, he pushed himself up from his mattress to see his dad collapsed on the floor. Ben jumped out of bed and bent down to help him up. Russell looked terrible. His face was drawn and had the yellow pallor of candle wax; his skin was moist with sweat. Ben put a hand to his forehead and felt that it was burning hot. He hooked his father's arms over his shoulders, then hoisted him up with all his strength and sat him back on the bed. Russell collapsed once more, heavily and without control, onto his mattress. He lay there for a few moments, his breath still rasping; this time Ben could also hear his chest rattling weakly.

His eyes were closed, but occasionally they would flicker open with difficulty and stare at the ceiling; then they would shut again. Ben had no idea whether his father was aware of his presence or not. 'Dad!' he said in an urgent whisper, not entirely sure why he was keeping his voice down. 'Dad! Wake up!'

Russell's eyes opened again, and he turned his balding head to look at his son. He smiled weakly. 'My head . . .' he murmured, before dissolving into a fit of hoarse coughing that seemed to jerk his entire body. As Ben watched his father struggling, an uncomfortable feeling crept over him. He had deteriorated impossibly fast overnight, and he didn't have to be a doctor to realize how likely it was that the ominous red cross might soon be being painted on the front door of their temporary home. He thought back to the previous night, to Halima's description of her parents' illness. The symptoms seemed identical, and his father had been down the mine only yesterday. 'Dad!' he whispered again. 'Dad, you've got to listen to me. I've got to tell you something.'

Russell's eyes flickered open and he looked blankly at Ben, who couldn't really tell if he was in a position to take in what he had to say. 'I'm ill,' the older man whispered. 'Malaria . . . I need medicine . . .'

'It's not malaria,' Ben told his father urgently.

Russell breathed out heavily. 'Ben,' he said wearily. 'This isn't the time. You've got to stop—'

'No, Dad,' Ben interrupted. 'I know what you're going to say, but you have to listen to me. Even the villagers don't believe it's malaria, and they should know – they've seen enough people dying of it.'

'Ben.' Despite the weakness of his voice Ben could hear his father trying to adopt that patient but slightly condescending tone he used when he was trying to explain something to his son. 'There are many different strains of malaria. Suliman told us . . .'

'I *know* what Suliman told us, Dad, but he's wrong. Think about it – we've only been in Africa for two days. What's the incubation period for malaria?'

Russell closed his eyes. 'A week to a month,' he said finally.

'Exactly. And anyway, you've been taking Larium for two weeks.'

Russell started to cough again, and Ben found himself wincing at the dreadful sound he made. He grabbed his hand and held it tightly, waiting for it to subside. Finally it did so, but it took a few more moments for Russell to summon up the energy to speak again. 'OK, Ben. Tell me what you think.'

Ben took a deep breath and started to speak. As he did so, Russell appeared to be trying to regulate his breathing, keeping it as measured as his weakened state would allow him. It clearly took a lot of effort: more sweat started dripping down his face, and his body started to tremble. 'Last night, while you were asleep, I went to the other side of the village with a girl I met. There was a ceremony of some sort, with a witch doctor and the village elders. They believe that the village is cursed because the miners have disturbed some ancient burial site, and that's why everyone's dying.'

'That's ridiculous, Ben.'

'I know, Dad.' In the depths of night and the strange surroundings, Ben had found himself half believing what Halima had told him; now, in the reassuring light of day, he knew that the sensible reaction of his scientist father was correct. 'But it's still true that it's the mine-workers who fell ill first, and that their families fell ill next. On our way back, we ran into Suliman. He was angry – angry with Halima, I think. Worried that she might have told me something.' He squeezed his dad's hand a little harder. 'And look at you now, Dad,' he said, his voice a little softer. 'You were only down there yesterday. We need to get you to a doctor.'

There was a silence between them, which Russell broke suddenly. 'Let go of my hand,' he hissed with surprising vigour.

Ben was confused.

'Let go of my hand,' Russell repeated firmly. 'And forget about the doctor for now.' His abdomen arched slightly as he tried to prevent another fit of coughing. 'Tell me more about what you've learned.'

'Not everyone gets it,' Ben told him. 'About two thirds of the mine-workers. And it's not' – Ben almost stopped himself, but an encouraging look from his father made him go on – 'it's not always fatal, Dad. Halima told me that only about three-quarters of the people who come down with the illness die.'

Russell gently closed his eyes, as though trying to come to terms with this information. Ben tried to think of something to say, but couldn't. It was his father who broke the silence. 'The bats,' he whispered.

Ben looked askance at him.

'A reservoir,' Russell insisted more strongly. 'They found a reservoir.' He dissolved once more into a fit of coughing.

'What do you mean, Dad?' he asked gently. 'Are you all right? Let me try and phone for a doctor.' He was worried that delirium might have set in.

'Listen to me, Ben.' Russell managed to sound impatient, despite his faltering voice. 'Have you ever heard of Ebola?'

'Sort of.'

'It's a virus – a nasty one. It's very rare, but the first outbreaks were found in this country, near the Ebola river. It causes death in most of its victims – horrible death.'

'What do you mean, Dad?'

'Fever, headache, nausea, then internal bleeding and haemorrhaging. Ebola sufferers start bleeding from every orifice and then, in most cases, they die within seven to fourteen days from multi-organ failure.'

Ben blinked as his brain struggled to decode his father's scientific language; but then Russell made himself plain.

'They bleed to death from inside and out. It's a terrible way to go.'

Ben felt his blood run cold. What his dad was saying vaguely rang bells with him: he had seen pictures in a Sunday newspaper supplement of people suffering from something similar. They'd had blood streaming from their nose and even seeping into their eyes; their skin had been covered with huge, weeping sores and welts. It was horror-movie stuff, but it was very, very real. 'Is that what you think this is?'

'No, Ben. No, I don't. Ebola only rarely transmits itself between humans. But it's not the only virus of its type out there, you can be sure of that. There's a similar strain of Ebola called Marburg that causes the same kind of symptoms; but the chances are that there are thousands of others, undocumented by humans, that have lain dormant for millennia.' Russell paused to catch his breath. 'When I was in the mine yesterday, I kept seeing dead bats.'

'I don't understand, Dad. Why's that important?'

'Viruses lie dormant in what's called a reservoir.'

'Water, you mean?'

'No, Ben. Listen to me. Not that sort of reservoir. A virus reservoir is an organism that plays host to the virus. It could be a plant, it could be an animal or a bird. Nobody knows what the Ebola reservoir is, but there is some evidence that it might be fruit bats . . .'

'. . . and you think the dead bats you saw in the mine were the reservoir for this virus?'

'No. The reservoir remains unharmed by the virus. I think these bats have disturbed something down there that is hosting the virus, and that they're now passing it on to humans. It's not Ebola, but if what you're telling me is correct, it *is* a viral infection of some sort; and if it's as contagious as it seems to be, it could be a hundred times worse than Ebola. We have to do something about it.'

'What *can* we do?' Ben's voice faltered as he spoke.

'This village is done for, Ben. Most probably I'm done for too. But if the virus is allowed to spread beyond here, there's no knowing what devastation it could cause. Millions of people could die. It can't be allowed to leave the village.'

Ben looked at his father in awed shock. He simply couldn't believe what he was hearing, couldn't believe that they had found themselves in this desperate situation. Then, in a flash, another thought struck him. 'They *know*,' he whispered.

Russell breathed out with a desperate shudder. '*Who* knows, Ben? What do you mean?'

'The mine-owners,' he told them. 'They've shut down the village. They won't even allow letters to leave – Halima tried to write to her sister to tell her that their parents were dead, but she didn't receive it.'

Russell said nothing.

'Don't you understand, Dad? If these people know about the virus, it means they're sending the villagers down there knowing full well what's going to happen to them. And if they don't want anyone to leave the village, that includes . . .'

Father and son looked at each other, waiting for Ben to finish his sentence.

'. . . that includes us.'

'Listen to me, Ben.' Russell's voice was getting fainter from the exertion of the conversation. 'Some people have an inbuilt immunity to certain viruses. That would explain why not everybody contracts the illness. Suliman and the other mine managers – my guess would be that they're immune. As for you . . .'

They looked at each other.

'. . . it's too early to say. You've been living in the same room as me for the last twelve hours. Even so, you should avoid contact with anyone else. And Ben.'

'Yes, Dad.'

'Promise me you won't try to leave the village. We need to get in touch with the authorities, warn them what is going on. If we don't, this could result in a natural disaster the like of which Africa has never seen. Do you understand?'

Ben nodded mutely, and his father collapsed once more in a paroxysm of coughing. When he had finished, he lay there in sheer exhaustion, his chest rattling, his breathing increasingly laboured.

He looked like a dying man.

Ben felt tears of frustration and despair welling up in his eyes, but he checked them almost immediately. There would be time for tears later; now he knew he had a job to do. Abele had told him that there was only one telephone in the village – a satellite phone in Suliman's office. He had to get there without being seen, and fast.

As if reading his son's thoughts, Russell spoke again. 'Take my business card from my wallet,' he panted. Ben turned and rummaged in his dad's bag until he found the wallet and removed it. On the business card was Russell's name and the number of the company in Macclesfield for which he worked. He hurried back to his father's bedside. 'There's a man there called Sam Garner. He's a friend of mine, an expert in infectious diseases. Speak to him. Tell him . . . tell him it's a Code Red. He'll understand. He'll know what to do.'

'All right, Dad,' Ben whispered. 'And then I'm going to find you a doctor.'

'No,' Russell said. 'Haven't you listened to what I've said? Nobody can come in or out of the village, not until the authorities get this thing under control.'

'But Dad, that could mean . . .' Ben couldn't bring himself to say it.

'I know, Ben.' Russell tried his best to smile encouragingly at his son. 'I'm just going to have to take my chances. We all are.'

Ben felt sick to his stomach. It pained him to admit it, but he would never have expected such bravery from his father. But then, what had happened to him in London and Adelaide had taught him that you never know quite what you're made of until you've got your back against the wall. He also realized implicitly that, even without the risk of contracting this dreadful virus, he was in a grave situation. If Suliman, Kruger and the rest of the mine-owners knew what was going on here, it meant they were willing to sacrifice scores of innocent lives to get their greedy hands on the Coltan down there. He had no doubt that their murderous ambitions meant they would not hesitate to silence Ben and his father permanently.

It was probably what they'd had in mind all the time.

And if that was the case, they wouldn't hesitate to stop anyone who got in their way.

Ben jumped up, motivated into action by a sudden thought. 'Halima . . .' he muttered to himself. He grabbed the gun from the table, checked the safety catch and slung it into his shoulder bag; he quickly pulled on the clothes that were lying in a heap by his bed, and placed the business card in the back of his combat trousers.

'I'll be back as quickly as I can,' he told his father directly, but his father said nothing.

Ben wasn't even sure if he'd heard him.

CHAPTER NINE

Ben sprinted across the main square to the top of Halima's street, but he was too late.

He could hear her screams even before he saw her. Staying out of sight with his back pressed up against the wall of another hut, he saw Halima being dragged out of her front door. Suliman was there, watching over three men whom Ben did not recognize – one of them had Halima's hair firmly clenched in his fist, the others were roughly jostling her. Even from this distance, Ben could recognize the weapons each of them had slung over their shoulders: AK-47 assault rifles, complete with fully loaded ammunition belts. Beyond them, parked at an angle across the dusty street, was an old beige Land Rover. The men started pulling the screaming Halima towards it.

Ben felt his hand reaching instinctively towards his shoulder bag and the gun that it concealed. The steel felt cold to the touch. Whenever he had held it before, he'd had no real intention of using it; the same could not be said now, and somehow that made the weapon feel heavier in his hand than it ever had done. He flicked off the safety catch and held it up. Suddenly his mouth was dry; he licked his lips to moisten them, then prepared to make his attack.

But something stopped him.

One of the men no longer had his Kalashnikov slung round his back; he was gripping it firmly and using it to prod the struggling Halima towards the truck. In an instant, Ben realized the truth of his situation: there were four of them, at least three of them heavily armed, and only one of him. And he'd never fired a gun in his life. He stopped in his tracks. Perhaps he should just slip away, do what his dad had told him and try and make that phone call. Suliman was diverted, and now would be a good time.

Then Halima screamed again, a terrified sound, and Ben realized he couldn't just leave her. He had to do something to help, and it would have to be something more subtle than just charging in there, inexpertly wielding a handgun. An idea formed in his head. It would be dangerous, but he could think of no other option.

Calmly he switched the safety catch on again, then tucked the gun into his combats, pulling his baggy T-shirt over the top to disguise its presence. Halima was almost at the Land Rover now, and Suliman was making his way towards the front passenger seat. Ben took a deep breath, then ran towards them.

'Hey!' he shouted. 'What are you doing? Leave her alone!'

Suliman, the three men and Halima all spun round to see Ben hurtling towards them, his arms waving in the air. He saw the girl shake her head, her desperation suddenly replaced by an urgent if silent warning for Ben to get out of there. The men looked less fearful; they sneered at each other, and then two of them raised their rifles in his direction. Ben skidded to a halt, feigning surprise, then spun round as though looking for an escape route. 'Put your hands on your head, Ben' – he heard Suliman's quiet, intent voice – 'and walk towards us, slowly.'

Ben did as he was told. As he approached them, one of the men walked towards him and then followed him from behind, prodding the AK-47 into his back. He carried on walking towards Halima.

'Empty your bag,' Suliman instructed. Ben did as he was told, silently grateful that he had hidden the gun under his clothes. The bag was empty.

'Get into the back seat,' Suliman whispered. Ben

felt the gun jab sharply into his back, and he stumbled forward. Halima was already being bundled into the back, and Ben scrambled in, taking his place next to her.

'You should not have come!' she whispered.

'I had to,' Ben breathed. 'I'll explain later.'

'Quiet!' Suliman was in the passenger seat now, directly in front of Ben, and two of his men had taken their places in the driving seat and the third seat in the middle. From the front, Ben could smell stale sweat and alcohol – someone had been drinking. He glanced out of the side window to see the remaining man step back down from Halima's open door, slamming it shut behind him. The engine started and the Land Rover skidded slightly as it set off and made its way to the edge of the village.

'Where are we going?' Ben asked tensely, watching Suliman's expressionless face jolting in the rear-view mirror on account of the bumpy road and poor vehicle suspension.

The men in the front remained silent.

'I know there's something down the mine,' he insisted, ignoring the hiss that came from Halima. 'My father fell ill this morning.'

Suliman smiled. 'That is good,' he said softly. 'It means there is one less of you to deal with.'

Ben felt a surge of anger welling up in him. The vehicle was moving quickly. There was no way they could safely jump out, even if they could have coordinated such an action without raising the suspicions of their captors; but the outskirts of the village had already melted away, and a mile after they left the last dwelling place, Ben realized he had to act now or not at all. Slowly, and as inconspicuously as he could, Ben reached his hand under his T-shirt and removed the gun from his jeans. The safety catch clicked softly as he undid it, but the sound was more than overwhelmed by the clattering of the Land Rover over the poor road. Halima's eyes widened slightly when she saw what he was doing, but she managed to suppress the gasp that rose involuntarily to her lips.

Now the gun was out, he had to move swiftly. He held it up and placed it directly to the back of Suliman's skull. 'In case you were wondering,' he said firmly, 'the thing you can feel is an automatic handgun. Tell the driver to slow down or I'll shoot the three of you – starting with you.' The aggressive words felt uncomfortable in his mouth, but he knew he had to keep up the pretence of confidence. Their lives depended on it.

Instantly the man in the middle started to raise the Kalashnikov that was resting on his lap. 'Tell him to put it down or I'll shoot,' Ben screamed.

Suliman shouted at his man in Kikongo, and he abruptly dropped the rifle. The driver looked nervously at Suliman, maintaining his speed and waiting for his instructions.

'Halima.' Ben spoke without turning his head to look at her. 'If he tells the driver to do anything except stop the car, tell me.'

Suliman's eyes narrowed, and he spoke shortly to the driver, who instantly slammed on the brakes. Everyone in the truck jolted violently forwards as the vehicle skidded through a right angle; Ben found himself hurtling forwards and to the side, his gun arm slipping past Suliman's head and into the space between Suliman and the man in the middle. Instantly Suliman's hand flew up and grabbed Ben's arm firmly.

Bang! The shock of his touch made Ben squeeze the trigger, and a deafening sound numbed their eardrums as the bullet ripped into the dashboard. But Suliman kept his grasp, squeezing hard and painfully while his accomplice slowly peeled Ben's struggling fingers from around the gun grip. The man caught it before it fell to the floor.

By now the vehicle was at a standstill, but pointing towards the side of the road. Suliman spoke briefly to the man sitting next to him, then let Ben's arm go and took the handgun from his accomplice before opening the door, climbing out of the front and getting into the back next to Ben. He held the gun firmly against his abdomen, then gave the driver a muttered instruction.

The Land Rover started moving again, straightening itself out before continuing along the road.

'You won't get away with this,' Ben told him. 'People know I'm here.'

Suliman ignored him.

'You need to listen to me,' Ben persisted. 'There's a virus down there. That's what's killing everyone. If you let it spread, millions of people could—'

'Speak again, Mr Ben,' Suliman interrupted him with a growl, 'and it will go very badly for you.'

They drove for twenty minutes. Ben stared ahead of him, his face fixed in an expression of the deepest contempt, and even though he didn't dare turn to look at her, he could sense that Halima was doing the same. He could sense Suliman too; he was close enough for him to feel the warmth emanating from his skin, and he could smell the sweat on his clothes. Ben was sweating as well, from a horrible mixture of humidity and fear. But most of all, he could feel the barrel of the gun bruising between his ribs. He did his best not to think about it, trying instead to come up with a way to get out of this. There *had* to be something he could do.

He could think of nothing.

One of the men in the front pulled a pewter hip-flask from his pocket and drank deeply from it. He offered it to the driver, who shook his head in annoyance. Around them the state of the road worsened, forcing the driver to reduce his speed somewhat, and the vegetation grew thicker: tall rubber trees started to line the road, forming an impenetrable wall of rainforest. There were no other cars. It all looked deeply inhospitable. At one stage the car slowed down as it negotiated a rickety wooden bridge crossing a wide river. The river itself was not very full – just a stretch of muddy-looking water slinking its way underneath them. Ordinarily, the treacherous bridge would have made Ben uneasy; at the moment, however, his mind was on other things.

Eventually Suliman spoke again, and the vehicle came to a halt. Still pointing the gun at Ben, he opened the door and climbed out. 'Get out,' he said flatly.

Ben and Halima did as they were told.

'Go round to the front of the car, face it and kneel down.'

By now the two other men were in the road. One of them had his Kalashnikov trained on them, so Suliman let the handgun fall and threw it onto the passenger seat. As Ben and Halima knelt down in front of the Land Rover, Ben could feel the scorching heat of the engine against his face. It gave him no warmth, though; his whole body had gone cold with fear. He knew what these men had in their minds.

One of them said something in Kikongo, and the others laughed. 'He wants to know which one of you will be first,' Suliman called out.

More laughter.

'Gentlemen first, I think,' Suliman continued. 'That is the British way, is it not?'

Ben's body shuddered. The man with the gun was behind him – he could tell by the scuffing of his feet in the dusty earth. But how far? A metre? Five metres? He had no way of telling. 'I'm sorry,' he whispered to Halima. Her breath was shaking and tearful. Ben glanced to the side to see a look of terror such as he had never seen before.

'Do it,' Suliman barked.

Ben clenched his eyes shut, every muscle in his body tensing.

Click.

He started, the shock of the sound forcing his body forward.

Click.

The sound again.

Ben and Halima looked sharply at each other, both realizing what it meant. The rifle had stuck: they had one chance to get away. 'Run!' he shouted hoarsely. The two of them stood up, spun round and barged their way past the man, who was looking at his weapon in confusion. Ben caught another whiff of alcohol – clearly the guy was too bleary to have cocked the gun properly. They sprinted down the road, and as they did so, Ben heard Suliman screaming behind them in Kikongo. 'We need to get into the trees,' Ben panted at Halima, loud enough for her to hear but not so loud that the others would know what they were planning. 'After three, bear to the left, OK?'

'OK.'

'One.'

Bang! A gun fired, and just ahead of them Ben saw an explosion of dust where the bullet fell.

'Two.'

He heard the three men behind them arguing and shouting.

'Three.'

Immediately they veered right, plunging under the canopy of the rainforest. It was unforgiving and barely penetrable, but they had no option other than to fight their way through. Back on the road, they heard Suliman furiously shouting something.

'What's he saying?' Ben asked urgently.

For a moment Halima didn't reply, too intent on fighting her way through the verdant bush. But eventually she spoke.

'Track them down,' she translated. 'And kill them.'

CHAPTER TEN

A couple of years ago, Ben's mum had taken him to Kew Gardens in London. A typical Bel Kelland day out, with lots of lectures about the environment and what we were doing to it. What he remembered most, though, was the Palm House, a huge glass pavilion in which the heat and humidity levels were high enough for all the exotic trees and plants that were kept there. It had been oppressive after only ten minutes; but it was as nothing to the surroundings in which he found himself now. His face was moist, not only from the perspiration of running, but also from the thick humidity in the air – ten times worse now he was under the canopy of the rainforest than it had been in the village. His unsuitable Western clothes were already ripped by the angry thorns of the unfamiliar plants all around him, their tough, juicy leaves barbed on the edge like the teeth of a saw. Remarkably he had not yet cut his skin, but he suspected it was only a matter of time.

Halima led the way, deftly finding paths through the thick foliage that Ben would never have seen. Behind them they heard the shouting of the men, seemingly coming from different directions but in fact, Ben soon realized, confirming the fact that he was wildly disorientated. He had no idea if he was running north, south, east or west. All he knew was that he had to keep going. They ran blindly for at least half an hour, both of them breathless and Ben feeling a sharp stitch in the side of his abdomen; he forced himself to push through the pain barrier, however, knowing that the alternative was a lot less palatable.

Eventually they stopped, spent a minute catching their breath and then, barely daring to move, listened around them. It was not silent. The screams of unseen birds filled the air; closer to the ground were the shuffles and movement of unknown creatures. But the sounds they were listening for – the shouts of their pursuers and the noise of humans inexpertly cutting their way through the forest – were absent. Ben looked at Halima in relief; her eyes were flashing darkly and she returned his gaze with a coldness Ben hadn't expected. 'You OK?' he whispered.

'No,' Halima replied sternly. 'This is all your fault.'

Ben blinked at her. 'What do you mean?'

'Those men, they would have never done this to me if you had not interfered.'

'What are you talking about, Halima? They were going to kill both of us.'

'You pointed a gun at them!' Halima started to raise her voice, only lowering it when she saw Ben wince. 'Do you not understand what that means in these parts? There are bandits everywhere – if you threaten to kill someone, they will try to kill you first.' Her Congolese accent could not hide her fury. 'Those men were taking me to the village elders. I was to be punished for showing you the ritual last night. Not killed.'

'No, Halima.' Ben spoke firmly, urgently. 'You're wrong. Listen to me carefully. Your village is *not* cursed.' She tried to interrupt, but Ben spoke over her. 'Let me speak. You heard me tell Suliman that my father has become ill – I have as much interest in this as anyone. He's a scientist – a good one – and he thinks that there is some sort of virus down the mine, highly contagious. The people who run the mine know this, but they stand to make a lot of money from the Coltan down there. Suliman knows we're on to them. I wouldn't mind betting that he has orders to kill anyone who discovers the truth. That's why he was abducting you – he thought I had told you what was going on.'

Halima looked confused.

'Think about it, Halima,' he urged. 'Why would the village elders send three men with AK-47s to catch a fourteen-year-old girl? It doesn't make sense.'

'No,' Halima said. '*You* don't make sense. If Suliman thought that there was a virus down there, why would he risk staying?'

'Because some people are immune. Like you, for example.' Halima's hand went up to the amulet round her neck, and she fiddled with it as Ben continued to speak. 'That's why they put Suliman and his men – people who they would never think of putting in positions of authority – in charge.'

For a moment Halima didn't reply, but eventually her wide eyes stared directly into Ben's. 'And what about you, Ben Tracey?' she asked in a low voice. 'Are you immune from this virus?'

'I don't know,' Ben admitted. 'All I know is this: if this thing spreads beyond your village, millions of people all over Africa could die. We have to alert the authorities, and we have to stop anybody from getting in or out until it's under control. We *have* to get back to Udok, Halima.'

Halima looked at him thoughtfully. 'You would

really go back, even though you believe what you believe?'

Ben closed his eyes momentarily. The image of his father, lying helplessly on his makeshift bed, appeared in front of him. 'I haven't got any choice,' he whispered, before looking back at Halima. 'You don't believe me, do you?'

Halima shrugged slightly. 'I believe something in the mine has been disturbed. You call it a virus, I call it something else. If your plan is to close the mine down, then we both want the same thing.' Her voice softened slightly. 'And I am sorry about your father. I understand what you are feeling. I will help you.'

'Thank you,' Ben said simply. He looked around him. 'We need to get back to the road.'

Halima shook her head. 'No,' she told him. 'It would be too dangerous. There are too many bandits in this region. If they saw us by ourselves, they would kill us just for the clothes we are wearing.' Ben remembered Abele's words of warning – *In the Congo, the only person safe from* voleurs *is the man with no money'* – and with a shudder he recalled the man who had tried to rob them when they first arrived in the region.

'You're right,' he said. 'And anyway, Suliman will be expecting us to find our way back to the road. I'd be willing to bet he'll have people there looking out for us.' It was a devastating thought. The canopy above was impenetrable, the surrounding rainforest dense and inhospitable. Ben felt something crawling on his skin; he slapped the side of his face to get rid of it, but could feel a mosquito bite already welling up there. With a sinking feeling, he realized that he did not even know in which direction they needed to travel to get to the village.

As though reading his thoughts, Halima spoke. 'The road we took travels in a straight line west from the village. We are somewhere on the north side. But if we are to travel east, we will have to cross the river at some stage.'

Ben nodded.

'It will be very dangerous,' she told him seriously. 'Many wild animals live in that river, and you do not always see them until they are upon you. Perhaps there is another way.'

'What?' Ben asked.

'There is another village twenty miles to the west of here. We would not need to cross the river. Perhaps if we could reach it, I could get in touch with my sister and ask her to raise the alarm.'

Ben shook his head. 'We might be carrying the virus,' he told her. 'We can't risk spreading it to anywhere else. Besides, it's too far. We need to raise the alarm as quickly as we can.'

'But the river—'

'Listen to me, Halima. The first thing Suliman will do when he gets back to the village is inform his superiors in Kinshasa about what has happened. They will suspect that you'll try and contact your sister. She's in great danger. If we don't raise the alarm quickly, who knows what will happen to her?'

Halima fell silent.

'I'm sorry, Halima,' Ben said after a moment. 'But you need to know what we're up against.' He looked around. 'I have to get to the satellite phone in Suliman's office, and I can't do it by myself.'

Halima nodded her head gently. 'Tell me what you want me to do.'

Ben chewed on his lower lip. 'The first thing we need to do is get our bearings,' he said almost to himself.

'I can use the stars to navigate,' Halima told him. 'But in here . . .' She looked up meaningfully at the thick canopy overhead. They were not going to see the sky for a while.

'Then the only other way I can think of discovering which way is east is by watching the sun rise.' Ben joined Halima in looking unenthusiastically up at the trees above him. 'We'll never be able to do that from here,' he murmured.

'There are hills in this region,' Halima told him.

Ben understood immediately what she was saying.

'If we can get above the tree line,' he mused, 'we'll be able to see the sun setting and rising.' He stood up. 'Let's get a move on. We still have armed men tracking us, so we need to go quietly.' A thought suddenly came to him. 'What are the chances of there being landmines in the forest?' he asked.

'Small,' Halima told him. 'Most people are not so foolish as to come here.'

Ben wasn't sure if that was a comfort or not.

He stepped away in a certain direction. Suddenly there was an unholy scream. It wasn't particularly loud, but it was full of terror and pain, causing the blood to run cold in Ben's veins and the birds in the trees to fly away in a deafening flock of movement. Ben stopped in his tracks and looked back at Halima. 'What was that?' he breathed.

Halima looked grim. 'It could have been anything,' she stated. 'One wild animal killing another, I think.' She stood up and approached Ben, who had changed from feeling forced confidence to sudden fear. 'There is only one way to survive in the forest,' she told him seriously, 'and that is to accept its ways. If you start to fear it, or break its rules, it will consume you.' She looked above her, where the birds were settling back down in the trees. 'Everything that happens here happens for a reason. If you understand that, all will be well.'

Ben took slow, deep breaths, listening carefully to what Halima had to say.

'Most of the animals here will fear us,' she continued. 'But if we impose ourselves upon them, they will have no option but to attack us. And if that happens, they will be far more dangerous than foolish men with guns.' She walked deftly past Ben and pulled back a curtain of palm leaves that blocked their way. 'Follow me,' she whispered. 'And go quietly.'

Ben and Halima struggled through the jungle in silence, heading uphill whenever the opportunity presented itself. By now it was midday, and even though they were protected from the direct beams of the sun, it was still growing intolerably hot. Already the inside of Ben's mouth was becoming dry and leathery; he kept it firmly closed in an attempt to prevent moisture loss, but he was still desperately thirsty. They would need water, and soon.

All afternoon they struggled. At times they would stumble upon natural clearings where ordinarily Ben would feel safer, relieved of the all-encompassing oppression of the rainforest; but they knew they could not stay long in the open. There were men after them, and they had to stay hidden. After a couple of hours, though, they found themselves on a steady incline, and at one stage they had to scramble over rocks to gain height. The low evening sun was blood-red in the sky when they found themselves on the bald summit, above the thick line of the trees. They sat there catching their breath, watching the sun slip easily across the sky. When it was threatening to disappear, Ben pointed in its direction. 'West,' he said shortly. 'Or near enough.' He stood up and turned round a hundred and eighty degrees. 'So we need to travel in that direction. Or as near to it as we can – it won't be easy keeping our bearings.'

Halima came and stood next to him, and for a few moments they looked in silence over the vast expanse of the African rainforest. It stretched as far as they could see, undulating and magnificent, punctuated in places by mountainous peaks, elsewhere by deep troughs that seemed to be filled with hazy steam. They could still hear the noise of the forest from where they were, but it was peaceful nonetheless. 'It is very beautiful, is it not?' she murmured. 'When men disturb what has been here for so long, no good can come of it. It is no wonder the ancestors are angry.'

Ben turned to look at her. 'It's not the ancestors, Halima,' he said gently. 'It's a virus.'

Halima smiled. 'You have great faith in your science,' she observed. 'But answer me this. If a snake bites you at your home, what would you do?'

'Find a doctor,' Ben replied. 'And fast.'

Halima nodded her head. 'It is true,' she said, 'that a doctor might be able to cure you. But would he be able to tell you why the snake bit you? Or what it was doing at your home? Or who sent it?' She looked back over the rainforest. 'Scientists do not know everything that goes on in this world.'

Dusk was falling, and Halima's words were disconcerting. 'We need to find somewhere to sleep,' Ben muttered to change the subject. 'Maybe we should stay here – nobody will be able to see us in the dark.'

'No,' Halima said. 'Animals will be here after dark. They will smell us, and we will be too exposed. And besides, it will rain soon. We do not want to be caught in it. We need to get back down, find some shelter.'

Ben took a final look across the trees into the African skies. 'Come on, then,' he said. 'Let's go.'

CHAPTER ELEVEN

They set up camp at the foot of a tall tree that Ben didn't recognize. It had large, flat mushrooms growing up the length of it like a spiral staircase, reminding Ben how hungry he was. Halima saw him eyeing the mushrooms. 'You are not thinking of eating them, I hope.'

Ben glanced guiltily back at her.

'If you eat plants you do not recognize,' she warned, 'you will do Suliman's work for him.'

'OK,' Ben said, a bit humbled. He knew he could last a long time without food; water, though, was a different matter. His throat was raw with thirst, and they would have to make it a priority tomorrow.

They sat in a small clearing, no more than ten metres wide. Clouds of insects swarmed in the air above him, and more than once Ben found himself slapping his skin to rid himself of a mosquito – real or imagined. He felt like things were crawling all over him. Now that they were not moving, the twilight crescendo of the wildlife around them became almost deafening. The chorus of cicadas formed a constant backdrop to the other sounds, which seemed to be reaching a frenzy before the setting of the sun finally robbed the rainforest of light: birds chirruping incessantly in the trees; monkeys screaming at each other; and the occasional more sinister sound – an unexplained rustle of the bushes, a rumble of something that could have been thunder but might have been something else, a dry hiss.

It was not cold, but Ben found himself shivering.

Suddenly he saw something. It may only have been a trick of the rapidly fading light, but it looked for all the world like a face, peering at him from behind a camouflage of leaves. Ben blinked, his stomach lurching. Was it one of the men? He had started to stand up before intuition got the better of him. If it was his pursuers, he would be dead by now. He looked at Halima, who was staring into space, hugging her knees; when he glanced back, the face was gone.

For a few moments he tussled with the idea of telling his new friend what he had seen, but he soon decided against it. It had probably been nothing, a

figment of his overactive imagination. And if not –
well, it clearly wanted nothing to do with them. No
point worrying Halima further, so close to night.

And then, as though someone had turned the lights
off, it became black; and as if at some prearranged
signal, the noise around them ebbed away. Now the
silent air was only punctuated by more alarming
noises – the occasional scream, or shuffle. 'We need to
stay close,' Halima whispered. 'Lie still, and don't run
away, no matter what you hear. If we lose each other
at night, we will never meet up again.'

And so Ben lay down. Underneath him was a soft,
mossy covering that made it not as uncomfortable to
lie there as he expected, but there was no chance of
sleep – at least not yet. At every sound his body
jumped, and the blackness all around him was so
complete it was like nothing he had ever experienced.
To keep track of time was impossible in such absolute
darkness, and Ben didn't even try as he lay there,
focusing instead on listening to the heavy sound of
Halima's breathing, and trying to ignore the itching,
crawling sensation that had started to cover his skin.
He wanted to ask her if she was still awake, but didn't
dare, for fear of alerting predators to their presence.
Occasionally the sound of breathing would disappear,
and in his night-time paranoia he would panic that
Halima had left him there alone; but then she would

start breathing heavily again, which at least came as some relief.

It was the other sounds that made Ben's blood run cold, though. Alien sounds. Inexplicable sounds. Some far away, others terrifyingly near. And all he could do was lie there, statue-still, and pray that whatever was making those noises would not detect their presence.

Eventually, however, after how many hours Ben could not say, the exhaustion of the day overcame him and he fell into a fitful sleep, his dreams haunted by images of his ailing father and the grim faces of the armed men, who he knew were out there somewhere. Searching for them. Ready to kill them.

At first, when he heard Halima's urgent whispering above the crashing volume of the dawn chorus, he did not know if it was a dream or reality. He lay there for a moment with his eyes closed, confused as to where he was and listening to her repeating the same words over and over again.

'If you are awake, Ben, whatever you do, do not move. Do not move, Ben.'

Ben opened his eyes and rolled his head to the side to look at Halima. She was precisely where she had been when night had fallen, lying on the ground just like him, but her gaze was directed between them, down towards Ben's leg. 'Whatever you do, don't move, Ben,' she reiterated.

'What is it?' Ben asked, even as he started to look in the same direction as Halima.

It took every ounce of self-control he had not to jump up in horror.

There, lying just below his knee, was a snake. It was coiled up and perfectly still, but the tail end of its body was draped over Ben's leg.

He froze.

'Two-step,' Halima said cryptically.

'What?' Ben breathed.

'Black mamba. We call it the African two-step. If it bites you, you take two steps and you—'

'Yeah, thanks, Halima,' Ben interrupted her. 'What are we going to do?'

'Do nothing. Now is the most dangerous time of day. It is cold and sleepy. If we disturb it, it is more likely to attack.'

Great, Ben thought. He closed his eyes.

'We need to lie still, wait for it to warm up. Hopefully then it will move away.'

'And if it doesn't?' Ben asked, but Halima did not reply.

They lay there in silence, neither of them daring to move. Around them the rainforest continued the process of waking up, but Ben paid it no attention; all he could do was focus on the gun-metal grey of the snake. Even though it was coiled up, he could tell it was long – a good two metres – and the end of its body started to feel heavy on his lower leg. He licked his lips, but his parched tongue felt dry against them. Almost as though looking in some grotesque mirror, he saw the snake's tongue flicker out. With horror, he realized that it was starting to move. Its head stayed flat on the ground and the coils did not change position, simply slinking round in a circle. The tail end slid off Ben's legs, which was a relief; but the head end was closer to them now, and there it stayed still.

Ben found himself transfixed by the terrifying sight of such a dangerous animal so close. It was impossible to tell by the sight of its beady black eyes whether it was awake or asleep, and the line of its jaw extended around almost the entirety of its almond-shaped head, giving the impression of a wicked smile. Again they lay there – for a few minutes or half an hour, Ben could not tell – but the sleepy mamba didn't move again. 'What do we do now?' Ben asked Halima.

'If we move, we need to do it very slowly,' Halima answered under her breath. 'And one at a time. If it senses movement from both sides, it may think it is under attack.'

'OK.' They were silent again for a minute. 'You go first,' Ben told Halima weakly. 'If it moves, I'll try to distract it.'

They looked into each other's eyes. Desperately

slowly, Halima sat up. The snake remained still. She got to her feet and started moving in a large circle around Ben and the snake, walking backwards so that she could keep tabs on what was happening.

Crack!

Halima set foot on a loose twig, and the sound of it breaking was like an electric shock through Ben's body. She froze, her mouth open in shock as they both waited for the snake to wake. But it didn't. Ben nodded shortly at her, and she continued moving carefully to the edge of the clearing.

Now it was Ben's turn. The mamba's head was a matter of inches from his right arm, and he felt that he had never moved so slowly or so quietly. Using his left arm, he pushed himself up from the ground, taking the utmost care not to lose his balance; if he fell on the snake, it would be the end of him. Once on his feet, he started to creep deftly away, choosing – unlike Halima – to keep his back to the creature.

He was almost side by side with her when she gasped.

Almost involuntarily, Ben spun round, just in time to see the mamba raising its body into the air. It must have been unbelievably strong, because by the time Ben had staggered back to Halima it was supporting almost its entire body weight so that its head was nearly a metre and a half above the ground. It wavered in the air, swishing delicately like a deadly pendulum. Ben felt himself being mesmerized by its stare; half of him wanted to turn and flee, the other half found itself rooted to the spot. The immobile half won the unseen battle, and both he and Halima remained locked by that venomous gaze.

Don't move, Ben told himself. If you move, it'll attack.

The snake began to hiss – not a single warning, but a sequence of repeated sibilance that sounded like it was working itself up to something. *Hiss . . . hiss . . . hiss . . .*

Stay where you are. If you turn and run, it *will* get you.

The hood around its neck started to flare up, its sleek head instantly becoming something much more sinister and aggressive.

And then it struck.

Ben saw it happen in slow motion. The snake's body coiled back, like a whip, before propelling itself through the air. He heard Halima scream and his own body went into a seizure of panic as the reptile flung itself towards them and downwards, finally coming to a stop on the ground half a metre in front of them.

There was a squeal. Ben felt his knees almost buckle as he saw the true object of the mamba's attention. A bush rat, furry and not much bigger than a fat hamster, convulsed in the mamba's jaws. The snake, firmly holding its prey, turned its head and slipped back to the far side of the clearing.

Ben and Halima turned to each other, nodded, and fled.

Chapter Twelve

Abele was troubled.

The mine-worker standing outside the entrance to Russell and Ben's compound bore a look on his face that made it quite clear he would allow nobody to enter. Abele didn't like the look of him. He wasn't Congolese, that much he could tell. Probably Rwandan, one of the many who had fled west across the border after the genocide. Many thousands of people had escaped to the Democratic Republic of Congo when the Tutsi extremists started massacring their Hutu neighbours, and the extremists too had crossed the border in order to escape justice. Consequently it was not uncommon to see Rwandan refugees all across the country, and it was equally difficult to determine whether they had fled justice or persecution. As a result the Rwandans were viewed with a certain amount of suspicion, even resentment. While the rest of the world looked on at the genocide in aghast horror, many Congolese remained un-interested. After all, they had their own horrors to deal with. Abele himself was one of the few people who didn't begrudge these people sanctuary, nor did he form unconsidered opinions about people; but even he had to admit that there was an arrogance to this man's demeanour that made him difficult to like.

Abele hadn't seen Ben or his father for two days now. It made no sense. Much as he didn't think Ben *should* go wandering around the village by himself, he knew that he probably *would*. But Abele had searched for him without success, which left three options: either he was being forced to stay in the compound, or he was ill, or something more sinister was going on.

He was a simple man – not stupid, just straight-forward. He had promised to protect these strange English people, and if there was a mine-worker stationed outside the compound, it meant Suliman had told him to be there. So he would ask Suliman. He would be able to explain what had happened.

Suliman's office was near the mine, just over a mile out of the village on the road heading east. Abele walked along the stony road, beads of perspiration forming on his face, until he reached the outskirts of the mine. Suliman's office was large by the standards of the village. It even had windows – not paned with glass, as this would cause the inside of the structure to become even more unbearably hot – but covered with a fine mosquito-proof mesh. The door was ajar, and Abele approached it purposefully, fully intending to barge in and demand what was going on.

But as he approached the door, he heard the sound of Suliman speaking in a raised voice.

The language was Lingala, the dialect more common further to the west of the country, near Kinshasa. Suliman was speaking hurriedly, as though he were trying to persuade somebody of something. 'Everything is under control,' he asserted.

Abele stopped by the door, something preventing him from entering. He stood with his back against the wall, listening carefully to what Suliman was saying.

'I already told you yesterday,' Suliman said in that characteristic half-whisper of his, 'that the scientist has confirmed the ore is good.' A pause while the person on the other end of the phone spoke. 'Well, if you need more confirmation, you will have to send somebody else. He has succumbed to the illness and he is raving. I expect him to be dead in less than a week.'

Abele's face hardened.

'No,' Suliman continued after a moment. 'They are

still unaccounted for. My men are tracking them, so they won't get far. If my people do not overcome them, then the forest will – they have no food, or water, or weapons. I don't expect to see them again.'

Abele muttered a curse underneath his breath. What was this fool thinking of?

'The workforce is thin,' Suliman was saying. 'Have you made arrangements for others to come? You realize that those who succumb will not survive long?' A long silence. 'No, Mr Kruger,' Suliman continued with a humility that sounded strange coming from him, 'I am not trying to tell you what to do. I will wait for them to arrive. Goodbye, Mr Kruger.'

Abele heard the phone being replaced in its cradle. What were these people up to? Why did they seem so worried about Ben and his father? Before he did anything, he needed to speak to Russell, to find out what was going on. As silently as his heavy frame would allow, he crept away from the open door and the office and started running back down the road towards the village. Had there been any camouflage, he would have made use of it; but there was none. He cut a lonely figure as he hurried along the road, unaware that from behind the mosquito-net window of the office, a solitary, dead-eyed face was watching him disappear into the indistinct haze of the distance.

He was drenched with sweat and humidity by

the time he reached the centre of the village. The Rwandan guard was still standing there, a look of bored insolence on his face, and he did not seem to have noticed Abele watching him from the other side of the square. Abele turned the situation over in his mind. He needed to get in there, to talk to Russell Tracey. There were two ways he could do it: over-power the guard, or create some sort of diversion. Abele was not a subtle man: for him, the best way was always the most direct.

He skirted round the edge of the square; he tried to look nonchalant, but it was not something that came naturally to him, so his thick-set features remained fixed in an unfriendly frown. The guard still did not seem to have noticed him, however, and remained oblivious to his presence as Abele approached him from the side. The Rwandan was not carrying a weapon – to do so would have been to cause consternation and gossip in the village, some-thing Suliman was clearly keen to avoid – so it would be a fist-fight, man against man. Abele's fists clenched as he got nearer, and he prepared to make his first punch a good one. Get him down before he had a chance to realize what was happening: it was the only way to ensure you would come out on top.

It was not until Abele was about two metres away that the guard realized something was afoot. Suddenly he became more alert, his casual slouch replaced with a wary, cat-like position, his eyes flashing cautiously and his lips curled into a patronizing sneer. He was a big man, his neck thick and his shoulders broad, but Abele was a match for him. And besides, he had the advantage. Using the full force of his weight, he pushed the guard into the compound, out of the eyesight of any interested passers-by. Once out of sight, he raised his knee sharply into the man's groin. The man bent over double in pain, and as he did so Abele jerked his knee up underneath his chin. There was a loud crack as the jaw crunched together and the man was propelled to the ground, landing heavily a good body's length away from Abele. He groaned as he tried to push himself from the ground, but a sound kick below the ribs soon made him collapse once more, and he fell into unconsciousness. Abele picked him up by the feet and dragged him across the ground to the edge of the courtyard. He tapped him sharply on the side of the face to check he really was out, and grunted with satisfaction when there was no response. Then he went in search of Russell.

Ben's dad was still lying on the bed. His lips were cracked and bleeding, and his waxwork pallor had given way to a jaundiced yellow sheen. Two days worth of grey stubble added a decade to his features. The room, Abele noticed, had the pungent smell of body odour that suggested that the heavily perspiring man in front of him had not moved for some time. 'Mr Russell,' he said gruffly, his voice low. There was no response. 'Mr Russell!' he said again, louder this time.

Russell's eyes flickered open and looked blankly at Abele. 'Ben? Is that you?'

'No, Mr Russell. It is me. Abele.'

Russell stared at him for some time, before closing his eyes again. 'Abele,' he murmured, the fact that he had finally recognized the man standing by his bed seeming to come as a great relief to him. 'I need some water.'

Abele looked around him. A half-full bottle of water was on the floor by Ben's bed, so he picked it up and gently trickled some of it into Russell's mouth. The white man tried to swallow, but the reflex had deserted him, and soon the water overflowed from his mouth and spilled down the side of his face. Abele stopped pouring, and Russell moved his moistened tongue around in his mouth. His eyes flickered around him, as though he was trying to work out where he was and what was happening. Suddenly everything seemed to come flooding back. When it did, he spoke. 'Don't touch me,' he whispered hoarsely, and clearly with great difficulty. 'Get out of here.'

Abele stayed where he was.

'You have to leave now, Abele . . .'

Russell spoke with all the urgency he could muster, but he was interrupted by the black man.

'Ben is in danger,' Abele said curtly. 'You are both in danger. What is happening?'

Russell was breathing heavily, almost gasping for air. 'The reservoir,' he choked, before his whole body was overcome by monstrous coughing.

Abele looked perplexed.

'Ben was just with me,' Russell struggled to say when the spasm had subsided. His eyes rolled in their sockets.

'No,' Abele stated. 'I have not seen him for two days. You are ill, Mr Russell. I think you do not know what you are saying.'

Russell pushed his tongue out of his mouth – Abele could see it looked furred and unpleasant – and used it weakly to lick his bloodied lips. 'How do you know Ben is in trouble?'

'I heard Suliman talking. He said his men were tracking him, but I do not know where.'

Suddenly Russell gripped the edge of the bed, and he held on as tightly as his weakened arms would allow. 'The room is spinning,' he muttered. He took some tremulous breaths before continuing his conversation with Abele. 'What else did you hear?'

'They are bringing more men in from the next village to work the mine,' Abele told him. He seemed about to say something else, but was interrupted by Russell's attempts to speak. What came out of his mouth, though, were not words but a garbled sequence of sounds. A blankness came over his expression, and he passed out.

'Mr Russell.' Abele spoke loudly so as to awaken him. 'Mr Russell!' But it was no good.

Abele thought for a moment. Apart from having established that Russell had succumbed to the illness, he was no wiser as a result of the conversation. He had no option but to confront Suliman. And quickly.

But he hesitated to leave.

His fingers reached inside his shirt and toyed for a moment with the shiny metal amulet that hung on the black leather thong round his neck. Almost instinctively, his fingers traced the indentation of the symbol it bore, round and round the shape of the eye as he seemed to be deciding something. Suddenly he clasped the amulet in the palm of his hand and pulled it over his head, before gently putting it round Russell's neck. The Englishman's skin felt burning hot to the touch. Abele muttered something under his breath, a chant of some sort, or a prayer.

And then he turned and left, feeling strangely naked, but knowing what he had to do.

CHAPTER THIRTEEN

'Stop running!'

Ben grabbed Halima by the arm and they came to a halt. Both of them were wide-eyed with shock, and Ben could feel Halima's body shaking. 'We can't lose our bearings,' he urged. 'The snake has gone. We *have* to keep heading east.'

Halima nodded vigorously, her face still displaying signs of panic, and the two of them looked around as they tried to work out where they were. 'This way, I think,' Ben murmured.

The direction in which he pointed was strewn with mossy boulders. There was no natural pathway as such, but it seemed for the moment as though they would be able to walk east without encountering foliage that was too impenetrable. They walked in silence, their encounter with the black mamba encouraging them to pay close attention to where they put their feet. Ben was glad he was wearing his reasonably robust trainers; Halima's worn sandals looked like they would afford her less protection if she put a foot wrong.

The trauma of the snake behind them, Ben realized how desperately thirsty he was. It had been twenty-four hours since he had drunk anything, and his parched mouth felt thick and leathery. 'If only it would start raining,' he observed half to himself.

'No,' said Halima. 'We don't want to get caught in the rains. They can be very fierce.'

Ben thought back to the incessant rains that had preceded the London floods. Something about the greenhouse-humidity of the air in the rainforest forced him to concede that a downpour here could be even worse than that. 'Whatever,' he murmured. 'Anyway, we need to find some water soon.'

Halima nodded, unconsciously licking her lips. 'But even when we find it, we need to be careful about what we use. Not all the water in the forest is drinkable.'

It sounded ominous to Ben, and he felt like changing the subject. 'You all right?' he asked. 'About the snake, I mean.'

'Yes,' Halima replied quietly.

'Pretty scary, huh?'

'Yes,' Halima repeated with an amused smile. 'Pretty scary.' The phrase sounded strange in her African accent. Then her voice became serious. 'The forest is a pretty scary place. How are you feeling?'

Ben understood what she was asking. They both knew that he had every chance of falling ill. Ben himself had tried to ignore that possibility, but it was entirely reasonable for Halima to ask. If Ben succumbed, she'd be on her own. 'I'm fine.' He smiled at her. 'So far.'

'Good.' Halima nodded in satisfaction. 'I think perhaps the ancestors are not angry with us.'

Ben opened his mouth as if to argue, but at the last moment thought better of it. Besides, there was something about what Halima had just said that made him feel a bit better about everything.

They continued to trek through the foliage.

Halima's face was a picture of concentration as they picked their way through the trees; Ben was concentrating too, not only on his surroundings, but on other things. Halima's question had brought to the front of his mind something that he had been trying not to deal with: the image of his father, weak and suffering. Possibly dying. With everything that had happened since he left the village, the horrible reality of his dad's situation had eluded him. Now, though, the facts of the desperate situation came flooding back to him, and it felt as though someone had thumped him in the stomach.

His dad was being so brave. Braver than Ben would have ever expected. He had to keep focused. Do what Russell had implored him to do. He had to make sure it wasn't all for nothing.

Suddenly Halima hissed, 'Stay still!'

Ben froze. He had been so resolutely checking his footing that he had momentarily taken his eyes off what was happening in front of him. Now he stood perfectly still as he took in the scene ahead. There was a clearing – more spacious than the one they had slept in that night, but not much – which at first glance appeared to be empty. Ben quickly saw, however, that it would be unwise to step into it. About five metres away, sitting quite still and eyeing them with a dis-concertingly human look in its eyes, was a gorilla. Ben returned its gaze, instantly realizing with something of a shudder that the face he had seen in the dying evening light the night before had been one of these creatures. The same one that was a short stone's throw away from him now? Perhaps, perhaps not. But the fact that one of these beasts had been watching them last night and had left them in peace somehow didn't make him feel much better.

And yet he knew that these were peaceful creatures,

as long as you let them be. He instantly suspected that these were eastern lowland gorillas, the endangered animals he had read so much about before coming. They were only to be found in these parts of the Democratic Republic of Congo, and were herbivores, living mainly off leaves. As if to confirm this information, the gorilla started chewing slowly, all the while keeping his eyes on Ben and Halima. You would be a fool, however, to assume that just because they were endangered herbivores they were not dangerous. These were the largest known primates – the males reaching a weight of up to two hundred and fifty kilograms – and they tended to live in small groups. These normally consisted of a silverback male, a couple of less dominant males and a number of females. With a squint, Ben saw the telltale white markings on the back of this huge mammal that indicated it was indeed the silverback. He would do whatever was necessary to protect the group.

There was a rustling in the bushes. Appearing with a surprising amount of grace for such enormous creatures, two other gorillas appeared, flanking the silverback on either side. Their huge domed heads and flat noses made them look terrifyingly aggress-ive, and they even seemed to jut their chins out pugnaciously.

Ben knew that he was privileged to be seeing what

he was seeing; but somehow it just didn't seem that way at the moment.

As though joined at the hip, Ben and Halima took a step backwards. The silverback continued to chew, seemingly unconcerned by the movement given that it was in the right direction, but keeping his eyes on the duo nonetheless. 'He's letting us go,' Ben breathed to Halima.

'We must move slowly,' Halima whispered. 'If we startle him, he will attack.'

Ben felt distinctly uncomfortable walking backwards, unable to see what was behind him, and acutely aware that he could be treading on anything – the image of the black mamba rearing above him was still fresh in his mind. But there was something about the magnetic gaze of the impressive creature in front of him that kept his eyes locked ahead. He almost felt a pang of regret as the gorilla slipped from his sight.

As soon as they were alone, Ben and Halima turned to look at each other. Halima made a circular gesture with her arm which Ben understood as meaning they should make their way around the group, if possible. He nodded his agreement and they quietly set off. As they skirted round where they believed the gorillas to be, Ben found himself almost breathless with excitement. Surely hardly anyone got as close as that to such magnificent creatures. He felt fortunate; he also felt as though the jungle had set them a test, and they had passed. What was it Halima had said? That there was only one way to survive in the jungle, and that was to accept its ways. If that was true, what had just happened was a good omen.

The thought made Ben smile. Omens? He was beginning to sound like Halima.

He put such ideas from his mind and continued to follow his companion through the forest.

Abele ran from the compound, ignoring the stares from passers-by as he did so. Perhaps Suliman would still be in his office, alone. That was just how Abele wanted him – unable to escape, unable to do anything except give him answers. His exertions, along with the increasing heat and the humidity, soon doused him in sweat, but he kept running, determined to find out what was going on, and to find it out fast.

He left the village and started on the long straight road that led to the mine. In the distance he saw the shimmering apparition of people coming the other way. They seemed to wobble and flicker in the haze of the heat, and at first Abele could not establish how many of them there were. Not that it matters, he thought to himself. There's only one person I'm interested in, and I know where he is.

Soon enough, though, the apparition became more

distinct. There were three men: two of them well built, the one in the middle tall but more slight. His head was shaved and his nose was long.

Suliman.

Abele soon saw that he was standing still, as though waiting for him in the road. The two men on either side of him stood slightly to the front. Unlike the man who had been guarding the Englishmen's compound, however, these two were armed – heavily. Kalashnikovs were strapped round their necks and ammunition belts hung loosely about their waists. Abele ignored them. His business was with Suliman himself, and he didn't intend to be intimidated by his crew. His broad brow furrowed and his shoulders hunched in anticipation of a confrontation, he headed straight for the unsmiling mine manager. 'Suliman!' he roared.

The men showed no flicker of acknowledgement, though they continued to stare at Abele, who marched inexorably towards them, violence on his face.

As he approached, however, Suliman's guards closed ranks. They aimed their weapons at Abele's torso, and barked at him in Kikongo to stop right where he was. Abele had no option but to comply. 'I am not afraid of your guns,' he said darkly.

'I can see that, Abele,' Suliman rasped. 'You are

obviously even more stupid than you look. Mr Kruger was right about you.'

Abele's face became filled with fury. 'What's going on?' he demanded harshly in the African dialect. 'What idiotic things have you been doing? Where is Mr Ben?'

'Why are you so concerned?' Suliman asked with a sneer.

'They are my responsibility,' Abele replied. 'I haven't seen Mr Ben for two days now, and I think you know what has happened to him.'

'You think too much,' Suliman snapped, his patience wearing thin, 'and you are not very good at it.' Then he smiled. 'You have sided with the wrong team,' he said smoothly. 'Your precious Mr Tracey is at death's door; his idiotic son will be waiting for him on the other side when he gets there. As for you' – his face crumpled up into a look of the utmost distaste – 'you seem to be little more than a slave to these white men. It would give me great pleasure to kill you now, so that you are waiting for them when their miserable lives come to an end. Fortunately for you, Mr Kruger wants to keep the unnatural deaths to a minimum.'

'Kruger.' Abele repeated the name with distaste, then spat at Suliman's feet. The bald man's eyes narrowed. 'It sounds to me,' Abele growled, 'as if the only slave round here is you. Kruger has you in the palm of his hand, eh?'

Suliman smiled. 'I'm being well paid for what I'm doing. That's the difference between you and me. And make no mistake, I have no qualms about silencing you if you force me to do so, no matter what Mr Kruger says.'

As he spoke, one of the guards threw him a questioning look. Suliman seemed to consider the unspoken query. 'No,' he said finally, his voice tinged with regret. 'Not here. Anyway, he might be useful. If by any chance the young people do make it back to the village, they will no doubt try to find this fool.' He sneered. 'They seem to have an adventurous streak. When they come looking for him, we'll just round them up.'

Suliman went over to one of his guards and gestured at him to hand over his Kalashnikov. The guard did as he was told while his colleague kept his own gun firmly trained on Abele. Suliman held the rifle carelessly and approached Abele. He poked the barrel of the gun firmly into the burly man's ribs. Abele stood tall, refusing to give Suliman the reaction he so clearly craved, so Suliman tried a bit harder, whipping the edge of the gun fiercely across the side of Abele's face. His head was knocked to the side, but he immediately turned it back to look straight at Suliman, displaying a thin streak of blood along the middle of his cheek. He stared balefully at his attacker, who could not stand that look for long and turned his back, handing the weapon back to his guard.

'Take him to the holding area I told you about,' he commanded, still failing to catch Abele's eye. 'Make sure there is someone watching over him all the time.'

Abele spat at him once more.

'And if he tries to escape,' Suliman continued in a deadpan voice, 'put a bullet in his skull.'

CHAPTER FOURTEEN

'They came this way.'

Suliman's men looked at each other. One of them was taller than the other, and his face had a pale scar reaching from his forehead to the top of his cheek. The other smaller man was distinguished by crooked yellow teeth that seemed precariously pegged into a set of red, sore-looking gums. 'Look here,' the taller man continued, pointing at where the foliage had been forced back to allow someone passage through. He pulled a small compass out of the pocket of his sleeveless shirt and checked his bearings. 'It looks like they're heading back to Udok.' He nodded with satisfaction. 'They'll have to cross the river, and the only place it's safe to do that is where it passes to the north of the village. If we don't catch up with them beforehand, we can deal with the idiots there.'

The smaller man sneered before pulling a water bottle out from his belt and taking a sparing glug. 'They're probably dead already,' he observed nonchalantly when he had finished. 'Only a fool would come into the forest without a gun.'

His colleague didn't respond.

'Come on,' the smaller man urged his friend. 'You know what they say about the forests north of the village. You don't want to find yourself there any more than I do. We should just return to the road, ambush a car and get back. Tell Suliman we killed them – he'll never know.'

His colleague seemed to consider that for a moment, but then shook his head in disagreement. As he did so, both men heard a low-pitched grunt. They looked sharply at each other, then simultaneously slung their Kalashnikovs round so that they were pointing in front of them; then they manoeuvred themselves to stand with their backs facing each other.

They heard the noise again, and movement in the trees beyond them.

'This way,' the taller man whispered. They walked side by side, stealthily, until it became apparent to them what was making the noise.

A gorilla sat, squat and alone, among the bushes a few metres away from them. It was not a silverback like the one Ben and Halima had encountered, but a young female, and she did not appear to be paying them any attention whatsoever. She reached out one of her arms and lazily plucked a handful of leaves from the surrounding greenery, then stuffed them in her mouth and started to chew, her hairy face gurning rather comically as she did so.

The eyes of the taller man narrowed. 'You want to see why I'm not scared of the forest?' he asked. 'It's because I have a gun, which makes me the strongest.' He licked his lips, then raised the rifle and took aim.

The gorilla looked up at him, but of course she had no idea what was happening.

When the man fired, it was as if someone had shaken the very roots of the trees. Birds screeched and flew away, and the aftermath of the shockwaves through the forest lasted long after the sound of the gun had ebbed away. As the frenzy of movement died, however, one sound remained. The gorilla had been knocked onto her back, a red welt on her left shoulder indicating the entry point of the ghastly wound that had just been inflicted upon her. She was making a series of pitiful yelps, as she clumsily tried to use her right hand to brush away the pain that she did not understand. It only took thirty seconds or so, however, for her energy to be depleted, and now she lay on the ground, her long arms listless beside her, her eyes flickering as she slowly began to bleed to death.

'You can't leave it like that,' the smaller man said. 'It's even more dangerous when it's injured.'

The tall man shrugged, then took aim again. The second bullet hit the gorilla in the head, and she lay still. He nodded with satisfaction that the danger they had encountered had been eliminated. 'Come on,' he told his colleague. 'We can't be far behind them.'

He turned and left the body of the gorilla, the smaller man following reluctantly behind.

'What was that?'

Ben and Halima had both stopped in their tracks at the sound of the loud bang echoing through the forest. Ben found himself breathing heavily. 'It sounded like a gun.'

'Suliman's men?' Halima asked.

Ben nodded. 'Probably. Whoever it was, I don't think we want to bump into them. We need to keep moving.'

They upped their pace, both of them casting the occasional nervous look behind them.

As the day wore on and the two friends grew more tired, the trees became thicker, the foliage denser and greener. It was impossible to move silently through such terrain and Ben found himself becoming accustomed to the swishing sound as the leaves brushed past his ears, and the occasional crunch as dead wood broke underfoot. Soon, however, he became aware of something else. A different sound. 'Stop a minute,' he said to Halima. They stood still, then smiled at each other as they both realized that it was the sound of running water. And it was close.

Their pace quickened, the prospect of quenching their thirst giving them a new energy. Suddenly they burst through the edge of the trees to find themselves on a wide river bank. Ben blinked as his eyes got used to the sudden light after the relative darkness under the rainforest canopy, his thirst forcing him to ignore everything around him other than the river ahead. The river itself was wide – too wide to cross, certainly – and fast-moving. Wild with thirst, Ben ran to the water's edge and bent down to scoop it up in his hands.

'Wait!' he heard Halima calling behind him.

Ben spun round to look at her. She was gesturing at him to walk back towards her; perplexed, he did as he was told. Suddenly he heard a sound behind him, and without knowing why he jumped away, further towards Halima. '*Attention!*' she shouted, lapsing momentarily into French. 'Be careful!'

When he finally turned round to see what it was, he

was very glad indeed that he had got out of the way.

Half in the water, half out, was a crocodile. It was small, perhaps only half-grown, but even without seeing its whole body Ben could tell that it was at least as long as him, if not longer. It lay there, dead still. Ben's heart stopped, and he found himself paralysed by the terrifying presence of the lizard-like creature, which seemed to be grinning at him, staring with life-less, flat eyes. Slowly, and without making any sudden movements, Halima bent down and picked up a long branch from the ground. She held it out towards the croc. 'If it attacks,' she whispered, 'we must go for the eyes. Or deep into the back of its throat, if that is what it comes to. They say that will make the jaws open.'

'They *say*?'

'Few people survive an attack from a crocodile.' Halima's voice was taut and tense. 'At least not from a full-grown one. This one is young. Maybe it is not so sure of itself. We are lucky.'

Ben didn't feel very lucky. He saw one of the crocodile's front claws moving slowly.

'The adults will not be far behind.' Halima scanned down the length of the river. A few hundred metres away, it curved to the right, but before it did so Ben could see with a squint that there was a herd of animals drinking from the waterside. From this distance Ben couldn't see what they were, but they looked from here not unlike young horses. 'See,' Halima stated. 'They come to drink where it is safe. We need to get there.'

They stepped slowly backwards along the river bank, Halima still keeping the branch outstretched towards the crocodile. Once they were a good ten metres away, and much to Ben's relief, the reptile twisted its body round and disappeared smoothly below the water. There was something about the way it moved that filled Ben with revulsion, and he found himself praying that they would not encounter another of those terrifying and deadly beasts. He glanced glumly across the water: there was no way of knowing what it was hiding.

The riverside was covered with smooth pebbles that crunched lightly underfoot as they made their way towards the animals that were still drinking by the water's edge. Ben's eyes kept flicking to the river to check for sudden movements, but he was also becoming increasingly intrigued by these horse-like animals. The closer he got, the more he realized they were not like anything he had ever seen. They were shorter in length than horses, squatter, and their backs arched upwards to make them look more like miniature giraffes than anything else. They were brown in colour, all apart from their legs, which had the characteristic black and white markings of the zebra. 'What are they?' Ben asked hoarsely.

'Okapi,' Halima replied, a mysterious smile on her face.

'What?'

'Okapi. It is rare to see them. Very rare. The men hunted them for bushmeat, and now there are very few left. But if they are drinking here, it is more likely to be safe for us.'

They approached the okapi tentatively. There were eight of them, standing in pairs. Insects, unrecognizable to Ben, were buzzing around their heads, but it seemed not to worry them. As Ben and Halima came nearer, a couple of them stopped drinking and looked in their direction, inclining their heads slightly and displaying no fear. Clearly they were as unused to humans and the harm they could cause as humans were to them. Ben and Halima stood quietly, waiting for the animals to become accustomed to their presence, which they soon did, bending down once more to continue drinking. Halima nodded at Ben. 'You sure the crocs won't attack us here?' he asked her.

Halima shrugged. 'Nothing is sure,' she said.

Typical Halima, Ben thought. But his throat hurt from dryness and his whole body was screaming at him to drink, so he and Halima took their places by the waterside to begin slaking their desperate thirst.

Ben cupped his hands and nervously dipped them into the water; it was cool and clear, and when he took his first gulps he could feel his body absorbing the precious liquid like a piece of blotting paper dipped into a bottle of ink. After that first taste, nothing could stop him and he abandoned caution as he drank deeply. It took at least ten handfuls of water before his thirst even began to be slaked, and he continued drinking for a long time after that, knowing full well that it could be some time before they found drinkable water again, and silently cursing that they had no means of carrying any with them.

When he could physically drink no more, he stood back from the river bank. The okapi had wandered further down, and Halima was sitting on a boulder, her face and hair wet, her eyes lingering on Ben. It struck him for the first time how pretty she was. 'Best drink I ever had.' Ben smiled at her.

Halima looked slightly bashful.

'I'm starving now, though,' he continued. 'Perhaps we could try and catch some fish?'

Halima's face became serious once more. 'I'm hungry too, Ben. Some fish would be good, and I know of berries we could collect; if we crush them and sprinkle them on the surface of the water, they will make oxygen and attract the fish. But I don't think we should risk it. I think we should get away from the river now. Crocodiles are not the only dangerous things that live here. And I have seen people being carried away just by the current near the village.'

Ben raised an eyebrow. 'You mean the river passes by where we're headed?'

'Of course. It is where the village gets its water.'

'Then why don't we just follow the bank? I know it probably meanders a bit, but wouldn't that be safer than risking losing our sense of direction in the rainforest?'

'No,' Halima replied shortly. 'I do not think that would be a good idea.'

'Why not?' Ben started to feel a sudden anger rising in him. Why was it that every time he suggested something, Halima shot it down in flames?

'Because I know the path the river takes, and our journey will be twice as long if we follow it.'

'But—'

'And because the rains are coming soon. Maybe today, maybe tomorrow. When they come, we do not want to be near the river. It will flood, and we will be carried away with it.'

Ben fell silent.

'Ben' – Halima looked honestly into his face – 'I am

not at home here. But I think perhaps I know the ways of the forest better than you, and I know what it will be like when the rain falls. You have to trust me.' She lowered her eyelashes a little. 'If it were not for you, I would be dead. I understand that. But we have to get away from the river. It attracts all kinds of animals, not just peaceful ones like these okapi.'

Ben knew she was right. 'I'm sorry,' he said. 'Come on, let's keep moving. We can't waste time getting back to the village.'

And so, slightly regretfully, they plunged back under the canopy of the forest and continued in what they hoped was an easterly direction.

The afternoon wore on, and Ben soon forgot the delicious sensation of not being thirsty as his mouth started to dehydrate once more. And as time passed, the sense of panic he had felt as soon as they had entered the forest started to increase. It didn't take much soul-searching for him to realize what was causing it. Darkness was approaching once more, and he did not relish having to spend another night in the pitch blackness.

Halima seemed to be more on edge too. 'Won't be long till dark,' Ben said to her, wondering if she was feeling nervous for the same reason.

She barely responded.

'What's the matter?' Ben asked.

Halima stopped. 'You will think I'm foolish.'

'No I won't,' Ben urged, unsure what she meant. 'I promise.'

Halima looked around her. 'If we are where I think we are, we will soon be entering areas sacred to the ancestors.' The noise of the forest seem to subside a bit as she spoke. 'They say it is haunted. I am afraid to spend the night here, but we have no other choice.'

Ben felt a coolness down his back, and he took Halima by the hand. 'We'll be all right,' he told her with a confidence he did not fully feel. 'We've been OK so far, haven't we?'

Halima smiled weakly, and it was obvious she was putting a brave face on her worries. They stood hand in hand in silence for a moment, each trying to derive some comfort from the presence of the other.

Suddenly there was a scream.

It was the scream of a man, and it was not far away.

Ben and Halima crouched down by the nearest tree. 'What was that?' Halima whispered, her voice wavering.

Ben was lost in thought. The gunshot earlier, now a scream. This was not a populated area – it could only be one of Suliman's men, and from what they had heard, it meant that they must be incredibly close. Every instinct howled at him to stay still, hidden; but perhaps there was another way. Perhaps that scream meant that one of them at least had met some misfortune. If that was the case, they might be able to take one of the Kalashnikovs. He understood what Halima had meant about respecting the jungle, but he would feel a lot safer with a gun in his fist. 'Wait here,' he whispered to Halima. 'I'm going to go and see what it was.'

'I don't want to stay by myself,' Halima breathed. 'I'm coming with you.'

As silently as they could, they set off in what they thought was the direction of the scream.

It only took a minute to discover what was going on. Hiding behind a lush thicket, they saw a clearing in the middle of which was a tall rubber tree. Daubed on the tree in orange dye was some kind of intricate symbol; and at the tree's foot, in a ramshackle pile, were the bones of an animal. In front of it, frozen with terror, was one of Suliman's men, unable to take his eyes off the symbol. His gun was strapped around his back.

Ben and Halima stayed perfectly still, scarcely daring even to breathe. As they crouched behind their camouflage, the second man – taller and with a nasty scar on his face – burst into the clearing from the other side. He spoke harshly to his accomplice in Kikongo, and the smaller man responded by pointing at the symbol and the bones.

The taller man gave him a look of disgust. He strode up to the tree, pulled a knife from his belt and hacked two savage cuts into the bark across the symbol. Then he kicked the pile of bones, scattering them around the forest floor, before speaking once more and dragging his friend away from the clearing and into the trees, unaware that their quarry was watching them only a few metres away. As he did so, Ben saw something fall to the ground.

They remained still and silent for several minutes, until the sound of the men moving noisily through the bush had long faded away. Only then did they dare speak. 'What was all that about?' Ben asked, his voice hushed.

Halima's face was shocked. 'It is a symbol of sacrifice.'

'A what?'

'Someone has performed a sacrifice to the ancestors here. A goat, probably.'

'But who would come all this way into the forest just to do that?'

'I told you,' Halima replied. 'This area is sacred to the ancestors. It would be a powerful spell to make a sacrifice here.'

'Then why was he so scared? What made him scream?'

Halima looked sombre. 'Perhaps because he knows

that what he is involved in is an insult to the ancestors.'

The two of them looked at the ramshackle pile of bones for a few silent moments.

'He dropped something,' Ben remembered. Gingerly, the two of them stood up and crept to the centre of the clearing. On the ground, just where the man had been standing, was a small pocket compass. Ben picked it up and used it to get his bearings. 'I think we've been going in the right direction,' he murmured, almost to himself. He flashed a momentary grin at Halima. 'Maybe your ancestors aren't such tricky customers after all.' He smiled. 'Maybe they've been giving us a helping hand.'

But Halima did not smile back. Her eyes were fixed on the symbol and the sacrifice. 'They should not have done what they did,' she intoned. 'Terrible things will happen to them. And to us, perhaps, for failing to stop them.' Ben instantly regretted his flippant remark.

She turned to him. 'Night is falling,' she said. 'I have no wish to remain here. Let us find somewhere else.'

Chapter Fifteen

Having already spent one night in the jungle, Ben was used to certain things: the increased activity just before nightfall, the sudden and relative silence once the light had faded. But nothing, he thought, would ever make him get used to the complete and utter blackness.

He was hungry too, he realized once they halted for the night. Achingly hungry. But he knew better than to suggest to Halima that they forage for food; if she had seen anything edible, she would no doubt have pointed it out. And Ben wasn't likely to start eating strange berries and vegetation out here without knowing what they were. He'd just have to get used to the constant clamours of his stomach for food.

As soon as the blackness descended, his ears

became superbly sensitive to every sound, and the dangers near and far became magnified in his mind a hundredfold. Every rustle was a silverback gorilla; every slither a black mamba rearing up to attack. He found himself unable to lie down, remaining instead in a sitting position, his arms held firmly around his knees.

'Are you awake?' Halima's voice was close and comforting.

'Yeah.'

Silence.

'Halima?' Ben said after a while. 'What was it like when your parents died?' As soon as he asked the question, he realized that it might have been some-what insensitive. 'I mean . . . you don't have to tell me if you don't want to. I just wondered.'

Halima thought before answering. 'It was like a night-time that did not end,' she said quietly. 'They suffered very much. You are thinking of your father, yes?'

'A bit,' Ben said in a small voice.

'He is not African,' Halima said with sympathy. 'My parents were thin and often ill. He is stronger. Maybe he will survive.'

'Maybe.' Ben had seen the desperate state his dad had been in before he left. He wasn't convinced. 'Do you think Abele will be OK?' he asked, to change the subject.

'If what you say is true, Ben, I do not think any-body will be OK.'

She was right. Even if they succeeded in raising the alarm – and that was a big if – the village would have to be isolated. Nobody would be allowed in or out until the virus had run its course, killing those who were susceptible to it, sparing those who weren't. Aside from being jungle-weary, Ben felt well enough; but he knew that that didn't mean a great deal.

'Abele can take care of himself,' he stated. Of that, at least, he was reasonably confident.

Abele was cold. He didn't understand why, as it was such a warm night. He watched his hand shaking in the dim light.

The wooden hut with its corrugated-iron roof in which he found himself would have been as dark as the rainforest had it not been for the smoky yellow light of a single candle. As night fell, Abele had thought it strange that he was being given this small creature comfort, but he soon understood that it was not out of concern for his well-being; it was so that, if they needed to check on him in the night, he would not be able to attack them under the cloak of darkness. If the glow of the candle from beneath the door disappeared, they told him, they would open up and fire randomly into the hut. And they said it like they meant it.

The door was locked – he knew that because he had heard the clunking of the padlock after he had been shut in – and he had heard the Kalashnikov-toting guard being relieved of his duty and replaced by someone else. How long ago that was, he couldn't tell. He knew there was no point calling out – down here, on the outskirts of the mine, there was no one to hear him – so he stood still, his brow furrowed in silent fury. Occasionally he would pace up and down the room to stop his limbs from becoming stiff. But only occasionally.

They would kill him sooner or later. He was sure of that. Suliman, that dog, had had a look of such contempt on his face that he knew he would take pleasure in doing it personally. He was only being kept here as bait – bait for Ben Tracey, who was up to something he didn't understand. He couldn't let it happen. If he was going to die, he wanted to die trying to escape, rather than on the whim of these men who had sold their souls to Kruger's wallet.

But that was easier said than done.

Abele enumerated his weapons. One candle, and the clothes he stood up in. It wasn't much, but slowly an idea started to form in his mind. It was risky. He might come off worst. But he had no other choice. He was desperate.

He removed his shirt, folded it neatly, then rolled it

into a tightly wound cylinder. He then unthreaded a worn lace from his prized but beaten-up leather boots and used it to tie the shirt in place. Picking it up, he saw with a nod of approval that it would not now unfurl. Then he moved over to the candle, took a deep breath and lit the end of the shirt. It started to smoulder and the acrid smell of burning cloth filled the hut. Gently, so as not to extinguish the small flames that had started to appear, he moved it over to the opposite wall, next to the door, and placed it on the ground.

The wood from which the walls were made had been baked dry by the sun. It wouldn't take long, he hoped, for it to ignite. Then he would be in the hands of the gods: either the guard would rush in and try to rescue him, in which case he would have to fight him for his life; or, more likely, the guard would leave him in there to die, in which case he would have to wait for the wooden wall to burn sufficiently for him to hurl his way through it. As long as he wasn't roasted alive first. Or suffocated.

The fire began to crackle and already Abele's eyes watered with the smoke. He ripped a piece of cloth from his thin trousers and placed it over his mouth and eyes, taking slow, infrequent breaths in an attempt not to breathe in too much smoke. Then he crouched down by the opposite wall, and waited. The wood was like kindling, and soon half the wall was covered in bright yellow fire. What Abele had not counted on, however, was the iron roof; it reflected the heat back into the hut like an oven, and within minutes he found himself clenching his teeth against the intolerable heat. He could not break out yet; the wall would still be too strong.

Just a few more minutes.

Outside he heard a shout of surprise from his guard, but it was difficult to tell what he was saying or how far away from the hut he was above the crackle of the fire. He realized that the padlock would now be too hot to touch, so there would be no chance of the guard coming in, even if he wanted to.

His skin was scorching.

He held his hand up to his hair; it was too hot to touch.

He couldn't bear any more of this heat. He was going to have to break out.

Just another minute.

The air burned the inside of his nostrils as he breathed in. He started to choke. There was nothing for it. It was now, or . . .

'*Aaaarrrggghh!*' he yelled at the top of his voice as he stood up and threw himself towards the burning sheet of flame in front of him. He felt the hot shock of a piece of burning wood splintering into his cheek.

His whole body shrieked with pain as his skin came into contact with the fire; but the wall gave way against his formidable bulk, and as he burst through, he heard the roof collapsing behind him. He was out.

The guard was only a few metres away, his face confused and his rifle trained directly at the door. When he saw Abele burst through the wall to the side, he shouted in surprise and turned his gun towards the roaring prisoner. But he was too late: Abele was upon him. His already impressive strength compounded by adrenaline, Abele knocked the guard's rifle out of the way; it fired a chugging round, but the ammo spat harmlessly into the burning hut. Still holding onto the barrel of the gun, Abele knocked it forwards so that the butt sank sharply into the guard's stomach. He spluttered, winded, before being floored by a brutal punch to the side of his face that exploded in a shower of blood the moment Abele's clenched fist connected.

He was out cold.

Abele pulled the Kalashnikov from over the guard's neck, then detached the ammo belt, moving quickly because he knew it would not be long before the burning hut served as a beacon to his accomplices. His hands were still shaking, and the rifle felt heavy in his hands. He aimed it at the man lying unconscious on the floor. One squeeze of the trigger was all it would take; one squeeze, and the man who would have killed him without a second thought would be with the ancestors.

Suddenly, though, the image of Ben popped into his head. The look of shock and horror that had crossed his face when he realized that Abele intended to kill the bandit who had attacked them the day he arrived.

Abele's lips curled into a sneer. He turned and left the man lying there.

It was a struggle to find the road that led into the village. Abele couldn't understand it – it wasn't like he didn't know the area well enough, but somehow he couldn't focus on where he was. He stopped for a moment and looked down at his arm. It was burning with an intense, white pain, and he could see a series of ugly burn blisters appearing along its length. As he looked at it, though, he felt his head spinning and a wave of nausea crashed suddenly over him.

The road, he told himself. I have to get to the road.

He looked around in confusion. 'That way,' he murmured under his breath.

By the time he reached the road, the nausea was all-consuming, making him forget even about the burns on his skin. He staggered along for perhaps fifty metres before he realized he could go no further. By the side of the road was a small copse of trees. He would be hidden there, so he stumbled towards them.

Immediately he was under their protection, though, he felt his legs buckle underneath him. He tried to take a deep breath, but he felt as though his airways were blocked. He coughed. A dreadful, racking cough.

A cough like the one he had heard coming from Russell Tracey, only a few hours before.

Ben awoke with a start.

For a couple of moments he looked around, not fully understanding where he was, confused by the ringing of the rainforest's early-morning noise in his ears. But then it all came crashing back.

Halima was stirring too; she opened her eyes and smiled at Ben, who was massaging a knot out of his neck and trying to forget about how hungry and thirsty he was. 'Bacon and eggs, anyone?' he asked with a sigh.

Halima looked puzzled. 'What is bacon and eggs?' she asked.

'Never mind,' Ben told her. 'Come on, we'd better get moving.' He consulted the compass and pointed in the direction they needed to go.

By mid-morning Ben started to notice that the foliage was thinning out a bit, and he had even seen a few stumps where trees had been hacked down. He gestured at Halima to stop. 'I guess this means we're getting close to an inhabited area,' he whispered. 'And we're less hidden now, so we need to be extra careful.'

Halima nodded her agreement. 'I do not think it is far to the river now.'

They continued to walk, their eyes darting all around them as they kept a lookout for Suliman's men. Soon, through a gap in the trees, Ben saw the twinkling blue of the river. He and Halima nodded at each other, then hurried towards it. As they reached the bank, Ben looked to the other side. Rising from the trees, a little distance away, he could see tendrils of smoke.

The village.

The place they were trying to get to; and the last place Ben wanted to be.

This time round, Ben knew better than to obey his body's urge to rush to the water's edge and drink. There were no animals sipping on the bank, and in any case there was less of a shoreline here, more of a mossy, treacherous bank forming a sheer drop down to the water. The river itself seemed stiller, calmer than it had further along; for some reason that just served to make Ben more nervous.

But as they stood there looking across, a horrible realization dawned on him. They had been so caught up in their desire to get to the river that they had not considered how they were going to cross it. Surely they couldn't swim – who could tell what dangers lurked beneath that still surface?

As though echoing his thoughts, Halima spoke. 'We need to find a boat.'

Ben looked left and right. There was no sign of anything. 'How are we supposed to do that?' he asked.

Halima shrugged. 'By looking.' She strode off along the river bank, with Ben following behind.

They spent the next half-hour searching along the bank for a boat. It was treacherous work, as they kept losing their footing on the mossy boulders, and all of a sudden the humidity had seemed to double in intensity. 'The rains,' Halima murmured at one point. 'We need to cross before they come.'

'Fat chance,' Ben said, knowing that he was sounding a bit surly. 'Look, Halima. Everyone lives on the other side of the river. Why would they leave a boat here—?'

He cut himself short as Halima looked at him triumphantly. There, a metre or so below the high bank on which they were standing, water lapping against its sides, was a small wooden boat. It was an insubstantial thing, rickety and unimpressive, but it was a boat nevertheless. Ben grinned as he felt relief surge through him.

It was short-lived. The instant his eyes fell on the

boat, he heard a shout behind him. He spun round and, a sickness rising from his stomach, saw the sight he had been dreading: Suliman's men, twenty metres away, emerging from the forest, their guns pointing in his direction.

'The boat,' he yelled at Halima. 'Get in the boat! Now!'

His shout was punctuated by the sound of gunfire. Half expecting that he had been hit, Ben grabbed Halima and they jumped into the boat. It was barely big enough for the two of them, and as they hit the decks it wobbled precariously, water sluicing in and settling in the bottom of the hull. There was one oar there; Ben grabbed it and used it to push against the bank as hard as his strength would allow. The boat shot out a few metres into the river before slowing down to a gentle drift as the pair flattened their bodies into the bottom of the vessel, vainly attempting to hide from the onslaught of bullets as Suliman's men fired at them from the river bank.

But the sound of bullets never came. Instead, there was a short, muffled scream.

Gingerly, Ben looked over the side of the boat towards the bank. What he saw, he knew he would never forget as long as he lived.

One of the men – the smaller of the two – was already down, floored by an enormous silverback gorilla who had evidently attacked them from behind. Now the gorilla was dealing with the taller man. With one swoop of his enormous arm, he sent him crashing to the ground. The man weakly tried to get up and gain control of his gun, but he was too slow; the gorilla was beside him, raising both hands into the air, then thumping them down with brutal efficiency onto the man's chest. Again and again he beat him, roaring deeply each time he did so and inflicting the blows so hard that blood started to explode from the unconscious man's mouth and stick to the animal's long fur.

The gorilla continued his work long after it was clear to Ben that the man was quite dead.

When he had finished, the silverback turned his attention back to the smaller man, pummelling him repeatedly to make sure he would never get up again either. And then, without even seeming to acknowledge the presence of Ben and Halima, he turned and disappeared into the bush, growling deeply as he did so.

Maybe Ben was fooling himself, but he almost thought the animal seemed satisfied with his work.

CHAPTER SIXTEEN

Ben and Halima sat up in the boat in shocked silence; the rainforest itself seemed hushed after that horrific display. Ben watched in distaste as three vultures, silently swooping down as though surfing on an invisible tide of misfortune, settled on the bodies of the dead men and started pecking small, red gobbets of flesh from their faces. He turned away, sickened, and tried to focus on something else.

Halima was right. The river was not as wide here as it had been at their previous stopping point; but it was still wide enough – forty metres, Ben estimated. There was a gentle current that was pushing them downstream, but it was not so strong as to make using the oar too difficult, so he crouched in the middle of the boat and paddled alternately on either side, careful to keep his footing and gradually inching closer to the far bank. The boat still wobbled treacherously, and it was all he could do to keep his balance. Halima seemed able to do nothing but stare at the dead bodies on the bank. 'I told you terrible things would happen to them,' she murmured.

Ben didn't reply.

It was strangely peaceful in the middle of the river. Ominously peaceful. The oars splashed regularly as Ben eased them slowly towards the other shore.

Splash.

Splash.

Bang!

Suddenly he felt something knock the boat. He lost his balance and allowed himself to collapse heavily into the hull in an attempt to stop from falling sideways. 'What was that?' he demanded, sudden panic in his voice.

Halima shook her head to indicate that she didn't know; as she did so, they felt the boat being knocked again. More water sloshed over the side, stabilizing it a little but pushing the rim of the boat down a little too close to the water for comfort.

And then they saw what it was that was knocking them.

At first it looked like an enormous grey boulder was

emerging from the water. It was Halima who realized what it was first. 'Hippo!' she gasped.

Instantly Ben grabbed the oar and, half kneeling, half standing, raised it up into the air to bring it sharply down on the head of the emerging beast. 'No!' Halima told him.

He looked questioningly at her as the hippo butted the boat once more, then allowed himself to sit down again as the vessel rocked dangerously.

'You cannot fight a hippo!' Halima told him scathingly. 'It is more dangerous than anything you have seen.'

'A *hippo*?' Ben asked, disbelievingly. But as if to back up what Halima had said, the boat was butted again, much more strongly this time. Ben and Halima grabbed firmly onto the side as it tipped almost to the point of capsizing – saved only by the fact that Ben had the presence of mind to hurl himself in the opposite direction and counterbalance his weight. 'What do we do?' They were both sopping wet and gasping for air, having swallowed large gulps of the river water.

'Hold tight and keep quiet,' Halima told him. 'Our only hope is that the hippo will leave us alone. If it thinks there is danger in the boat, it will continue to attack and that will be the end of us.'

Ben nodded, and the two of them lay down in the

pool of water that had collected in the hull, their clammy bodies pressed together as they clutched tightly on to the edge of the boat.

The vessel swayed sickeningly, still reeling from the last knock. With every moment that passed, Ben expected to be hurtled down into the water. He knew he could probably swim to the other side if that happened, but he had no idea what horrors would try to stop him if he ended up in the water. And then there was Halima. 'Can you swim?' he asked her.

'Ssshhh!' Halima reprimanded him, before adding, quietly, 'No.'

Great, Ben thought to himself.

They continued bracing themselves for another knock.

But it didn't happen.

'I think it's gone,' Ben whispered. Slowly he pushed himself up, his hands splashing in the water that had collected in the hull. He looked around him. Everything was calm – there was no sign of hippos or anything else. As he looked around, the hippo emerged once more, but further away from the boat this time. It was heading towards the far shore, towards the place Ben and Halima wanted to get to. But there was no way they could follow; Ben saw that now. 'I'm going to let the current drift us downstream a bit,' he told Halima. She eyed the hippo as it waded out of the water on the other side and nodded her agreement.

The current seemed slow, but in fact it didn't take long for the boat to drift to a point where the hippo was out of sight. Squinting at the other side, Ben thought he saw a suitable place to land, so he carefully knelt up once more and started paddling again, while Halima attempted to bail out some of the excess water.

They continued like this for a couple of minutes.

It was just as Halima had her hands over the side that she suddenly screamed. Quick as lightning, a crocodile had risen to the surface and snapped hungrily at Halima's arms. It was twice the size of the younger croc they had seen earlier, its skin horny and green-grey, and it was ten times more aggressive. Halima pulled back just in time, and the crocodile made another attempt, this time splintering the side of the boat with its razor-sharp teeth.

'Get back!' Ben shouted. This time he knew he had to do something; the crocodile was attacking, and clearly wouldn't just slip away like the hippo had. Adrenaline burning through his veins, he whacked it on the head with the flat part of his oar.

It did nothing. The croc attacked once more, splintering another part of the side of the boat.

Halima screamed again. Ben felt like screaming too,

but what would that do? He hit the crocodile for a second time, gagging as the smell of rotting flesh from its teeth reached his nose.

It just seemed to make the vicious reptile more angry.

The third time Ben hit it, he managed to get the eye, but the oar was too flat for him to be able to poke it properly. He started to panic. One more bite of the side of the boat, he reckoned, and they would start to sink.

Ben's head started to spin, and he found himself hyperventilating. His instinct was to grab Halima, to protect her from the crocodile's next attack, though what he really thought he could do he didn't know. The beast had submerged itself somewhat, and there was a terrible silence as the pair watched its massive body curl round and swim away. For an instant Ben felt shuddering relief, but that soon disappeared as he realized what the croc was really doing.

It was preparing for another attack.

Ben knew what crocodiles did – it was the stuff of playground horror stories. Once it had one of them in its jaws, it would disappear with them to the bottom of the river until the struggling had stopped. Then it would store them in an underwater hiding place until the meat was slightly rotten before eating it.

It seemed to happen in silent slow motion. The

water above the animal parted as it headed towards them, picking up speed as it came and opening its mouth, gaping wide.

One snap of those jaws and they would be crocodile food.

It was two metres away. Ben raised his oar.

Just as the crocodile was upon them, there was another movement in the water. For the second time in only a few minutes, Ben saw the boulder-like hump of a hippo emerge to the side of the crocodile. With surprising speed for such an ungainly animal, the hippo opened its lumpy jaws. The hippo's teeth were not as numerous as the crocodile's, nor as sharp; but they were huge and strong, like elephant tusks. As they closed round the body of the crocodile, the reptile started flailing in sudden pain and panic. Its lizard-like tail swung up in the air, showering Ben and Halima with a torrent of water. When they had wiped their eyes, they were only just in time to see the hippo submerging itself, its almost dead prey still clamped firmly in its prehistoric jaws.

There was no time to be relieved. The bulk of the hippo and the frenzied wriggling of the croc had caused the still water to become treacherous; and the holes the reptile had ripped into the side of the boat were allowing water to gush inside. Ben plunged the oar back into the river, and with all his might started sculling towards the bank; but they were sinking fast. It was clear they weren't going to make it.

'We're going to have to swim!' Ben shouted.

'I cannot!' Halima cried.

Ben sized her up. She was about his height, but slighter of frame. It was perhaps fifteen metres to the shore; he was going to have to carry her. It was that or let her drown.

Quickly he pulled his saturated shoes from his feet, and with all his strength threw them to the shore. 'Give me yours,' he told Halima; when she did so he threw them ashore too.

They had less than a minute before the boat was completely submerged. A sudden calm fell over Ben; he knew exactly what he had to do. He crouched down. 'Climb on my back and hold onto my shoulders,' he instructed Halima, whose eyes were now wide with fear like he had never seen. She did as she was told. 'Not so tight round the neck,' Ben said. Halima loosened her grip, but only slightly. Neither of them said what they were both thinking: that there could be anything between them and the shore. They were just going to have to trust to chance.

Ben had intended to hurl himself from the boat – that would have given him an extra couple of metres' start; but suddenly he became aware that the bottom of the hull had disappeared from beneath his feet.

Halima's weight sent him under, and he kicked as hard as he could to bring them back up into the air, where they both spluttered. Then he started to swim.

The current was stronger than he had anticipated now that he was in the water, so he had to head on a diagonal towards the bank. The strain of going against the flow, together with the weight of Halima behind him, meant that soon the muscles in his arms, along his back and into his legs were burning with exhaustion. Every few strokes he would find himself going under, and he had to gather all his remaining strength to push the two of them back up to the surface of the water.

Ten metres to go.

Five metres.

The pain in his arms was too much. He was sinking. He did his best to gather his energy for one final surge up above the water, but it simply wasn't there. He was going down. He closed his eyes and held his breath.

And then his foot hit the bottom of the river. It felt hard, stony and slippery beneath him. Halima was wriggling and struggling on his back, but she kept holding on tight – too tight, around his neck. Ben looked up and opened his eyes to see sunlight stream-ing through the surface of the water. It was close. They couldn't be far from the edge now. Battling against the current, he took a step through the water. It was like wading through treacle, but somehow he managed it. And then another step. And then, if he stood on tiptoes, he could just get his head above the water. He gasped loudly, filling his air-starved lungs with a deathly rasp.

Halima was still on his back, so her head was already above water. 'Put me down,' she ordered. 'I can walk from here.'

Ben did as she said. And then he made the mistake of looking behind him. His eyes just above the level of the water, he could see the telltale mounds of crocodiles in the middle of the river, like floating logs. 'Hurry up,' he gasped. 'We have to get out of the water.' They waded towards the shore, urgently trying to get there as quickly as possible, but frustrated by the resistance of the water. It seemed to take for ever.

Gradually, though, the water became suddenly less deep, and they were able to run out, desperate to put distance between themselves and the circling crocs, despite the fact that the stones were cutting into their bare feet. Quickly Ben gathered their shoes; but once he had done so, he felt his legs collapse, jelly-like, beneath him. He was dizzy with exhaustion.

But Halima would not let him sit down. She started pulling at his arm: 'We have to get away from the river, Ben. The crocodiles are coming!' Ben looked out over the water to see she was right; the mounds were not so far away now, and getting closer. He forced himself to stand up, and then the two of them ran, still holding their wet shoes, behind the trees that lined the river.

The forest was less thick here, and if Ben's body had not been so desperately tired they could have run faster. But after a couple of minutes he could go no further. 'Stop!' he tried to say; but all that came out was a hoarse, high-pitched wheeze. Then he bent over and, unable to help himself, started to retch.

He would have been sick, but there was nothing in his stomach to come up.

CHAPTER SEVENTEEN

It took Ben a good fifteen minutes to recover. He sat on the stump of a felled tree, struggling for breath and bent double with pain. Halima sat on a stump too, her wet hair sticking to the side of her face as she gazed at him with a kind of wonder.

Eventually Ben found his voice. 'You OK?' he asked weakly.

Halima nodded with a mysterious smile. 'Yes,' she said. 'I am OK. Thanks to you.' Her eyes seemed to bore straight into him.

Ben found his face reddening, and he was suddenly overcome with the urge to change the subject. 'I wish we could find some dry clothes,' he said, looking down at himself so as to avoid Halima's gaze. The sunlight beneath the trees was too dappled, and the humidity was too intense, for them to dry off.

Halima smiled. 'It will rain soon. Then we will be even wetter, if we do not reach the village beforehand.'

'We'd better go then,' Ben agreed. He forced himself onto his feet, and was alarmed by how stiff his muscles were. Best to keep moving, he thought to himself. If I sit here for too long, I'll never get up.

There was no road as such leading to the village, but Halima led the way confidently enough. Ben tried to ignore the wetness of his shoes, which were causing blisters on his skin as he walked, and it was with a certain sense of satisfaction that he saw the trees thinning out even more. 'Here,' Halima said finally. She sounded subdued.

Ahead of them was a clearing. It was deserted, but it was obvious that there had recently been activity here. It was surrounded on three sides by trees, although on one of those sides the greenery had been crudely hacked away to make room for a rough dirt track. A long pile of earth was mounded up alongside a wide trench; parallel to these were other trenches that had clearly been recently filled in. Ben felt sick as a realization gradually dawned on him – a realization that was confirmed when Halima spoke. 'My mother and father lie here,' she whispered.

Ben looked at her in horror. 'Is this a mass grave?'

Halima nodded mutely, her jaw clenched.

'Why?' Ben breathed.

'I told you, the people from my village are dying quickly. There is not the time or resources to make separate graves for them all.'

Suddenly there was a noise beyond the trees: a vehicle. Ben and Halima scurried to hide behind a bush, and from their hiding place they looked out on to the grave. An old truck trundled up the path, coming to a halt at the top of the trench. As he watched, Ben felt a horrible premonition of what was to come, but somehow he couldn't turn his eyes away. Two men climbed out of the truck, opened up the back and strained as they pulled off a body, one holding the shoulders, the other holding the feet. From this distance Ben couldn't tell if the corpse was male or female; but he could see the skin was black. He felt a sense of guilty relief: it wasn't his dad.

The two men returned to the back of the truck and pulled off another body. Ben blinked, and a shudder passed through him.

It was a body of a child.

The tiny corpse was given no more ceremony than the one that went before; it too was slung into the deep grave, before the men pulled a pair of shovels out of the back of the truck and started to cover the latest occupants in loose dirt. It looked like back-breaking work – clearly the bodies needed to be well covered in order to stop wild animals from digging them up. Soon, though, their work was done and they drove off.

When Ben turned to look at Halima, her face was grim. She muttered something to herself in Kikongo.

'What did you say?' Ben asked.

Halima shook her head. 'It doesn't matter,' she told him.

Ben felt a surge of sympathy for her. What must it be like, he wondered, to know that your parents were rotting in an unmarked grave, just two out of count-less forgotten corpses? 'We're going to put a stop to this,' he said calmly.

'How can we?' Halima's eyes were distant, and she spoke as though she had lost hope.

'By stopping the spread of this vi—' He cut himself short. Halima didn't believe in the virus, not really. But she knew the mine had to close. 'Listen, Halima,' he said, slowly and patiently. 'I have to make this phone call to England. It's the only way the mine is going to be shut down. And you know it *has* to be shut, don't you?'

Halima nodded.

'Good. Because if it isn't, this won't be the only mass grave in your country. There will be thousands of them, in every town and every village. It could be a disaster like the world has never seen. Trust me, I know a thing or two about disasters.'

He let that sink in for a moment.

'Shall we go?' he continued.

Halima smiled thinly as she nodded her head. 'Yes, Ben,' she said. 'Let us go.'

They saw nobody as they hurried away from the graves. Hardly surprising, Ben thought. It's not the sort of place you want to hang around. 'Do you know where Suliman's office is?' he asked after a little while.

'Yes,' Halima stated. 'It is by the mine, not far from here. But his men will be all around – we will not be able to get there without being seen. And what if he is in his office?'

Ben's eyebrows furrowed. Halima was right, of course. They had been concentrating so hard on getting to the village that they had not devised any kind of plan to get to the satellite phone. 'Let's cross that bridge when we come to it,' he said, a bit unconvincingly.

The decision was upon them sooner than expected. Before long they found themselves skirting the edges of the mine. It was busy: dejected-looking workers were trudging around, and guards with the now-familiar AK-47s seemed to be everywhere. It looked to Ben like an impossible situation; as soon as they stepped out into the open they would be seen. And shot, most probably.

Ben chewed on his lower lip in worry. 'What are we going to do?' he whispered to Halima as they crouched down together behind a low bush.

As if in answer to their question, Ben heard a low rumble in the near-distance. It sounded strangely out of place here. 'Was that . . . ?'

A broad smile spread across Halima's face.

'Thunder,' she confirmed. 'The rains are coming.'

'We need to find shelter,' Ben worried.

But Halima was still smiling. 'No,' she said. 'It is not us who will find shelter. Watch.'

Ben could scarcely believe the speed with which the skies darkened. There were no rolling clouds, just an all-pervasive gloom that seemed to stick to everything.

And then it started to rain.

At first the drops were infrequent, but strangely heavy. They splatted on the dusty earth like bullets. Ben watched in wonder as all the men drifting around the mine seemed to disappear into huts and shelters.

Soon enough he saw why.

Ben had never encountered rain like it. It gushed from the sky like a waterfall in the air. Within minutes the dusty roads had turned to fast-moving streams, and their clothes were as heavy with water as they had been when they came out of the river. Rain streamed down their faces and crashed noisily around them. Halima pointed at a hut that was larger than the others. 'That is Suliman's office,' she screamed, struggling to make herself heard above the noise of the rain.

'OK,' Ben yelled back. 'Let's go!'

As the first heavy drops of rain fell upon Abele's face, his sore eyelids opened with difficulty.

It was day now, and the light seemed to pierce his eyes right through to the very centre of his skull. His body was shaking violently, and his stomach was knotted with nausea. He had no idea how long he had been lying there, nor did he feel in any state to move.

Then it all came flooding back: Russell Tracey, Suliman, the fire. People were in danger. He had to do something.

He struggled weakly to push himself up from the ground, wincing as his burned hands scraped against some jagged stones. Once he was on his feet, he had to grab hold of a nearby sapling to steady himself. The world seemed to spin and he nearly collapsed into a shivering pile; but somehow, something kept him going and he staggered back onto the road. The rain was falling heavily now, so heavily that it seemed to bruise the top of his head, and as he stood there, soaked to the skin, he became aware of his heavy breathing, rasping and gasping. His mind was disorientated and he looked in confusion around him, unable to work out which direction led to the village and which back to the mine. He chose a direction at random – minewards – and staggered along the road. Occasionally he fell and had to push himself back up again, his face grimacing and muscles straining. It was the hardest thing he had ever done.

Both the rain and the illness blurred Abele's vision, so he could not be sure, once he had covered the short distance to the mine area, that his eyes were not deceiving him. He blinked and looked again: it certainly seemed like them. Ben and Halima were rushing across the empty ground, their hands covering their heads to protect them from the pelting rain. They headed towards Suliman's office, then looked furtively around before sneaking inside. What were they doing? Abele tried to make his brain work, but it was spinning and confused. He tried to call out to them, but his voice failed him and he merely doubled over in a fit of coughing. As he straightened up, he lost his balance and fell to the ground, facing the opposite way, back towards the village.

Again he blinked. There was a Land Rover on the road, travelling slowly because of the rain, with its headlights on full beam. It was heading straight for Abele who, rather than move out of the way, simply sat there staring, unable to force his body into action.

The sound of the rain blotted out the noise of the vehicle's engine until it was nearly upon Abele; by the time it was that close, he became aware of the fact that the horn was beeping loudly. The Land Rover stopped a few metres away, waiting for him to shift out of the way, the horn continuing to honk; but Abele just stayed where he was, unable to move. The windscreen wipers swished furiously, but still the heavy rain made it impossible to tell who was in the vehicle, and no doubt the driver had just as much difficulty seeing out.

Eventually the door opened and someone emerged. He was tall and lanky with a pronounced Adam's apple and a shaved head. Abele looked up at him in distaste. 'Suliman,' he spat with difficulty.

Suliman gave a nasty sneer and spoke to Abele in Kikongo. 'So that's where you've got to after last night's heroics. It looks to me like you'd have been better off where you were.'

But Abele wasn't really listening to him. The image of Ben and Halima rushing into Suliman's office flitted once more through the confused jumble of his mind. He didn't know what they were doing, but he was sure it would go badly for them if Suliman discovered the two youngsters in his office. He had to stall him. Give them time. If it was the last thing he did.

'Get out of the way,' Suliman was saying.

Abele just stared at him, unable even to shake his head. He didn't move.

'I told you to get out of my way,' Suliman insisted, his voice threatening.

Abele stayed right where he was. He didn't know what Suliman would do, but he just kept his mind focused on one objective: to make sure Ben and Halima had enough time.

The rain continued to fall on the two men.

When it became clear to Suliman that Abele would not budge, he nodded firmly to himself, then disappeared back into the car, returning a few seconds later with his assault rifle. Grim-faced, he pointed it at the kneeling Abele. 'Get out of the way,' he ordered for the third time.

Abele slowly raised his eyes, looked into Suliman's face, and shook his head.

Instantly, Suliman whacked Abele on the side of his face with the rifle. It was a vicious blow, and it caused Abele to topple heavily onto his side, a deep gash across his face. The rain washed the blood onto the ground below him, and Abele's eyes flickered closed. Then he heard Suliman's voice. 'I could kill you now if I wanted,' he boasted. 'Nobody would know, and nobody would care. But I choose not to, because you're going to die anyway, and it will be far more horrible than the easy way out of a bullet in your skull. That's what has happened to your friends, by the way – the girl and the young English boy.'

The rain pounded on the side of Abele's face, stinging his cut.

Suddenly he felt his ankles being grabbed and he was dragged unceremoniously to the side of the road and into a ditch. The wet dust scraped along his face, yet he still couldn't find the energy to open his eyes, let alone fight back. All he could do was hope he had stalled Suliman for long enough.

Suliman himself looked down at the prostrate figure with distaste. He spat at him, then kicked him hard in the stomach before turning back, sodden and scowling, to his truck, leaving Abele in the ditch to die.

The noise of the rain against the corrugated-iron roof of Suliman's office was almost deafening.

The moment they were inside, Ben looked around for the satellite phone. He found it soon enough, on a table in the corner. It sat in a hard, black flight case with a separate, bulky battery on the floor and a wire leading up the wall and through the roof – to the antenna, Ben assumed. The rest of the table was a mess of wires and plugs, and Ben realized he had absolutely no idea how the thing worked. 'Keep watch out of the window,' he told Halima. 'Let me know if anyone comes.' Then he turned his attention back to the phone.

The handset was large and bulky, with a small LCD screen at the top. It was attached to the main body of the apparatus with a curling black wire, but there was no response from the buttons when Ben pushed them. He directed his attention to the battery and saw a red switch. He flicked it and the LCD screen burst into life.

The number. With a sinking feeling, Ben realized he had put it in his back pocket, and since then he had not only been swimming but had also been totally soaked in the rains. Gingerly he felt for the card his dad had given him. It was still wet, so he pulled it out as gently as he could for fear of ripping it. Ben could hardly bear to look at the thing, so sure was he that it would be unreadable. He breathed out explosively when he realized that the phone number of his dad's office in Macclesfield was still legible. Sam Garner was the name of the guy Dad had told him to call, and when he spoke to him, he knew he would have to sound convincing. Very convincing.

'There is a car coming up the road,' Halima told him, her voice tense. 'Hurry up.'

Ben nodded efficiently, then dialled the number. He strained his ears to listen to the ringing tone; it wasn't easy above the pounding of the rain on the rooftop, and even when the tone arrived, it was weak and crackly, occasionally cutting out. Ben listened, silently praying for his call to be answered.

Ring-ring.

Ring-ring.

It seemed interminable.

Ring-ring.

Ring-ring.

'Pick up, pick up, pick up,' Ben whispered to himself.

Ring-ring.

'Sam Garner.'

The man's voice sounded distant and distracted. Ben's mind went blank – how was he going to explain to this guy what was happening so many thousands of miles away? How could he make it clear how desperate the situation was? 'Mr Garner,' he said briskly, 'this is Ben Tracey. Russell Tracey's son.'

There was a pause. 'Hello, Ben.' Garner sounded confused. 'Is everything OK? I thought Russell said you were going with him to Africa.'

'I was. I mean, I am. That's where I'm calling from. You have to listen to me.'

Silence.

'Mr Garner, are you there? Can you hear me?'

'You broke up for a minute there, Ben. It's not a

good line. You sound worried – what's the matter?'

And then the words came tumbling out of his mouth. 'Dad's ill. I think he might die.'

'Ben,' Halima said urgently. 'There is somebody getting out of the Land Rover. I think it is Suliman. And there is someone on the road in front of him. I cannot see what they are doing – the rain is too bad.'

But Ben was talking over her to Garner. 'We're in a tiny village called Udok in the Democratic Republic of Congo, and half the village is dying too. Dad thinks it's a virus – like Ebola, only worse, more contagious. The reservoir is down the mine he's been investigating. He thinks that if anyone gets in or out of the village, it could spread quickly. You have to get in touch with the authorities, make them seal the village. You *have* to let them know how important it is. Dad said you were the only person he knew who would understand. He told me to tell you it's a Code Red scenario.'

By the time he had finished his piece, Ben's voice was cracking with exhaustion and emotion. He waited for a reply from Garner, but there was none.

'Mr Garner? *Mr Garner?*'

Ben felt a sickening lurch in the pit of his stomach as his ear was filled with a continuous high-pitched tone. The line had gone down. He cursed the weather under his breath.

'He is getting back into the car,' Halima said. 'We have to go.'

'No,' Ben said, even as he dialled the number again. 'I got cut off. I don't think my message got through. I'm going to have to try again.'

'Hurry up, Ben. He will be here any minute.'

Stony-faced, Ben kept the handset to his ear. All he could hear was the continuous tone. He tried again. Same thing.

'It's the weather,' he said almost to himself. 'Must be.'

Who else could he call? Who else would take him seriously? His mum, of course. He felt his fingers instinctively dialling her number, but again he heard nothing but the incessant, high-pitched tone.

Ben hadn't minded getting caught when there was a chance of him getting his message through, but now he suddenly realized he couldn't risk it. He turned to Halima. 'Come on, let's go. I'm going to have to try again another time. Let's get out of here before Suliman gets back.'

He carefully placed the handset back into the flight case, and the two of them slipped back out into the pouring rain. Suliman's Land Rover was approaching, but the lie of the land was such that it was not pointing directly at them, so he and Halima remained unnoticed by the mine manager as they sprinted back to the cover of the trees.

Seconds later, Suliman arrived at the hut. He parked the truck outside, then hurried in out of the rain, carelessly carrying his AK-47 and muttering under his breath at the stupidity of that idiotic man Abele. He was beginning to have second thoughts about his actions – maybe he should have just killed him when he had the chance. But Kruger had wanted suspicious deaths kept to a minimum, and who was he to argue with the man who was paying him so well?

In his anger, he failed to see the wet footprints on the floor. And as he started stripping off his wet clothes, he failed to see two figures running as fast as they could down the road that led to the village.

CHAPTER EIGHTEEN

As Ben and Halima hurtled down the road in the gushing rain, they didn't notice Abele, unconscious in the ditch by the side. Nobody noticed them either – there was no one about, as everyone was taking shelter from the elements. It was only when they reached the compound that they stopped, taking cover for a moment under a corrugated-iron canopy. Their sopping clothes stuck uncomfortably to their skin, and Ben felt the cold pain of physical exhaustion deep in his chest. The two of them stood there, breathless, and Ben found himself suddenly reluctant to go in. He surveyed the square in front of him. Through the pouring rain he could see, on the other side, a body lying on its back. It was on some sort of makeshift stretcher. 'Look,' he said to Halima, pointing in the direction of the body. 'They must have been taking him away to the burial site when the rains came.'

Halima nodded mutely.

Ben's edginess increased. 'We should go over there and move him out of the rain,' he said.

'And what would that do, Ben?' Halima asked, giving him a piercing look.

Ben shrugged. 'I don't know. I just thought . . .'

But he stopped talking and looked down to his side, where Halima had taken his hand.

'You are scared to go in to see your father because you fear what you will find there,' she observed.

Ben winced slightly, and nodded his head. 'What if he's dead?' he asked plaintively.

Halima gave him a sympathetic look. 'I understand,' she said. 'If you would rather I stayed out here . . .?'

Ben thought about it for a second. 'No,' he said finally. They had been through a lot together, and for some reason he now drew a kind of comfort from her presence. 'No, come in. If you want to,' he added.

He took a deep breath and led the way.

From the doorway, he could see that his father had not moved in the time Ben had been away. He was still lying on the bed, deathly still. Ben felt suddenly sick; from here his father did not seem to be breathing. He exchanged a worried glance with Halima.

And then there was a sound: a long, drawn-out breath that seemed to last longer than any breath Ben had ever heard. It did not sound good, but at least it was a sign of life. He rushed to his father's bedside.

'Dad?' Ben said tentatively, not wanting to shout but struggling to be heard above the sound of the rain. 'Dad, can you hear me?'

For a few seconds there was no response, but then Russell's eyes flickered open. He almost seemed to recognize his son, but just when Ben was about to speak again, his father's eyes fell shut once more.

Ben put his face in his hands. He couldn't bear to see his father this way.

'Ben?'

He looked up sharply. Russell's eyes were open again.

'Ben,' he whispered hoarsely. 'Is that you?'

Ben nodded.

'Oh, thank God,' Russell murmured. 'Abele said you had disappeared.'

There was no point, Ben thought, explaining where he had been. 'I'm here now. You need water,' he told his dad, looking around and seeing his bottle of water where he had left it. He held it to his dad's lips, and his father seemed to derive some relief from the liquid, though he appeared to have lost the ability to swallow and the water did little more than sluice out from around the side of his parched and bleeding lips.

'Did you call Sam?' Russell asked.

'I tried to, Dad. I spoke to him, but I'm not sure the message got through. The line was bad – I'm going to have to try again, but Suliman is in his office now and I'll have to think of a way to lure him out.'

Russell coughed weakly. 'Never mind that now,' he said. 'Where's Abele?'

'I don't know. I haven't seen him.'

'He was here,' Russell breathed. 'I don't know when – maybe yesterday. He told me that . . .' Again he dissolved into a fit of coughing before he could continue speaking. 'He told me that they are bringing workers in from the nearest village.'

Ben blinked as the implications of that news hit home. This was exactly what they wanted to avoid.

'It's starting, Ben.' His father seemed to echo his thoughts. 'It will only take one of those people to return to their home carrying the virus, and nobody will be able to stop it spreading. You *have* to make sure it doesn't happen.'

'How am I supposed to—?' Ben started to ask, but he cut himself short as his father emitted another of those deathly rattles from his lungs. 'Dad, are you OK?' he asked urgently.

But there was no reply. Russell Tracey had slipped once more into unconsciousness.

Ben bit his lip. All he wanted to do was to stay here, to look after his father. But that was not what his father had urged him to do. Gradually he became aware that the noise of the rain hammering on the roof had stopped, and Halima had approached and was standing just behind him. 'What should we do?' she asked.

Ben closed his eyes and breathed deeply and slowly in an attempt to regain his composure. 'Where is the next village?' he asked quietly.

'West of here,' Halima said. 'On the road Suliman took with us.'

'Is that the only road in?'

Halima nodded.

'And how far away is it?'

'Half a day's drive. Maybe a day because of the rains.'

'OK. There might still be time.' He chewed thoughtfully on the nail of his right thumb. 'I've got an idea,' he said. 'This is what we're going to do . . .'

Four thousand miles away, the same sun that was once more emerging over the rainforests of the Democratic Republic of the Congo was also beating down on the city of Macclesfield in Cheshire. Sam Garner, a bearded, bespectacled man in his mid-forties wearing a rather unfashionable short-sleeved shirt and a tie with soup stains down it, was glad of the air conditioning in his offices; but he was deeply concerned by the phone call he had just received. He had never met Russell Tracey's son, and didn't know if he was the sort of kid to pull practical jokes. But if his father was anything to go by, somehow he doubted it.

Sam had called the operator to try and trace where the call had come from, but there was nothing she could do to help. The more he thought about it, the more firmly he decided he had to take it seriously. It was too outlandish for a kid to make up, surely, and Ben had sounded genuinely fearful. But who should he call and who would listen and, even more importantly, be able to *act* on such meagre information? He twiddled with his pencil and tried to think things through calmly and logically. Sam Garner had seen the effects of the Ebola virus first-hand. He'd researched a small outbreak in the Central African Republic about three years ago, and he remembered thinking how much worse these diseases were in real life than in academic study. The people he had seen dying of the virus had ended their lives in terrible pain. At the time he remembered being thankful that you could only catch Ebola if you came into contact with the bodily fluids of infected sufferers. Humans had never caught it through airborne transmission, though monkeys possibly had. A slight mutation, and Ebola could turn into a health threat the like of which the world had never seen.

It had become something of an obsession of Sam's. There was no doubting that there were millions of organisms out there unknown to modern science, microscopic bacteria and viruses living in tiny un-discovered colonies with their own quirks and characteristics. You didn't need to be an amazing scientist to work out that with so many millions of possibilities, it was not only *likely* that someone some-day would stumble across a new virus as invasive as Ebola but much more contagious. It was *inevitable*. Sam had even developed his own system of grading virus threats.

Code Green: no threat.

Code Amber: discovery of reservoir and suspected threat to human life.

Code Red: widespread infection and threat of major epidemic.

Sometimes Sam's colleagues made fun of him and the way he had taken to lobbying governments and NGOs, getting up on his soapbox and arguing the need for more funding in this arena; but Sam didn't care. He knew what he thought, and he knew one day he would be vindicated in some horrific way.

Perhaps that day had come. Or perhaps Russell Tracey and the villagers of this unheard-of place in the DRC had succumbed to something totally different. All Sam knew was that what Ben had described was perfectly possible, if unthinkable, and that Russell Tracey was not the sort of man to overstate his case. If Russell thought this was a Code Red situation, it probably was.

But his thought processes simply led him back to square one: who would be the best person to notify? Who might act promptly based on no real data? But if this really was a Code Red . . .

He had an idea. Clearing an unruly pile of papers from his desk with a sudden sweep of his arm, he pulled the keyboard of his computer towards him and directed his Internet browser to a search engine with a light tap of his fingers. Within seconds he had directed himself to the United Nations website. His eyes scanned quickly over the screen until he saw the link he was looking for: 'PEACE & SECURITY'. He navigated to the peacekeeping section of the website, then found the link for 'CURRENT OPERATIONS'. A drop-down menu directed him to 'AFRICA' and then 'MONUC (DEM. REP. OF THE CONGO)'. A few clicks later, he found himself scribbling down the number of the main office in Kinshasa of the UN Mission in the DRC.

Then he stopped.

What were they going to think, these people, when he phoned them out of the blue to alert them to a deadly virus in an unheard-of backwater of the country? What would *he* think, if someone he had never heard of called him up to say that half the population of Britain might die if he didn't quarantine Macclesfield? If ever there was a long shot, this was it. Sam Garner knew he was going to have to be *very* convincing.

He dialled the number.

'*Oui, bonjour,*' a woman's voice answered almost immediately.

'Do you speak English?'

'Yes, sir, a little.'

'Good.' Sam spoke slowly and clearly. 'My name is Dr Sam Garner. I'm calling from England and I am a specialist in infectious diseases. You're going to have to listen to me *incredibly* carefully . . .'

CHAPTER NINETEEN

'When will you be coming home, Daddy?'

The thin child who looked up at her equally emaciated father was eight years old, with large dark eyes and tightly curled hair. She didn't want her father to leave.

'In two weeks,' he said gruffly, softening only when he saw the tears welling up in his daughter's eyes. He knelt down and took her hand. 'The men say there is work in the next village. When I come back, I will have a little money. Enough, maybe, to buy some meat for us. You must look after your mother while I am gone. Do you think you can do that for me?'

The little girl nodded bravely. Her father smiled at her, stroked the side of her head, then stood up. His wife was standing in the corner of the hut, obscured somewhat by the shadows. He nodded cursorily at her, then left.

Outside, the minibus was waiting. It was an old bus, like every vehicle the man had ever seen, with rust patches and mismatched wheels. And it was almost full. He hurried towards it, not wanting to risk missing his seat. The smiling men who had flown in from Kinshasa the previous day had told him that this was a limited opportunity for work, that if they wanted to earn some of the money that was available, they needed to sign up now and leave tomorrow. Little did anyone know that they would be back to transport another busload of workers as soon as possible.

Quietly the man took his place at the front of the bus. It was hot and smelly, and filled with men who, like him, had faces that reflected the hardship of their lives, yet now showed hope that they might be able to earn the money they so desperately needed to support their families.

That had been this morning. They'd expected to be in Udok by lunchtime, but the rains had come, holding them up. Now they trundled along slowly, all of them anxious to be at their destination.

None of them, of course, had heard the rumours. There were no televisions in this part of the world, no newspapers. Half the men in the minibus did not even know the name of the village they were going to.

And none of them knew what they were letting themselves in for . . .

The first thing Ben and Halima needed was an axe.

Halima had suggested that there might be one near the mine – the workers were forever clearing trees to make room for new excavations – but Ben wasn't keen on the idea. The rains had cleared, and although the paths and tracks were still deep with puddles, the villagers had come out from their huts. The last thing Ben wanted was for them to be seen by Suliman and his men. Not yet, at least.

'There is a man who lives near me,' Halima told him. Then she corrected herself. 'I mean, he *lived* near me. He is dead now, along with his family. But he used to cut wood. His hut is deserted, but I think we might find something there.'

The pair kept their heads down as they crossed the square, doing their best to remain inconspicuous but acutely aware of the fact that they had no time to lose. At least, Ben thought, they had one thing in their favour: the area round Halima's house always seemed to be deserted, and if the inhabitants of the hut they were heading for were dead, there would be a red cross on the door and people would be avoiding the place anyway. Sure enough, when they got there, nobody was around.

The door was locked. Ben sized it up and decided that it looked flimsy enough. 'Stand back,' he said to Halima, before stepping back a few metres and then running at it with his left shoulder. The door rattled a little, but it didn't give way, so Ben tried again. Only on the third attempt did he break in. They rushed inside.

The hut was dark and unwelcoming. A couple of old, thin mattresses that had seen much better days lay on the floor, and there was a table and two chairs. All sorts of other paraphernalia of daily life were littered around, and Ben and Halima immediately set to work trying to find what they were looking for.

It didn't take them long. A heavy-handled axe was lying on the floor, its blade covered by an old rag. It was Halima who found it, and she tried to pick it up, with difficulty. It was a very weighty thing, and even Ben didn't feel like he could carry it for too long. If only Abele were here, he thought to himself.

But Abele wasn't there, so they were going to have to make do by themselves. 'I can't carry this all the way up to the mine,' he told Halima. 'It'll just get in the way. We're going to have to hide it somewhere and pick it up later.'

They left the hut, Ben dragging the axe behind him, and headed for the road leading west.

Once they were on the outskirts of the village, Ben started looking around for a suitable hiding place. Finding somewhere to secrete the axe wasn't a problem – there were plenty of low bushes that would have concealed it – but ensuring that he could locate it again was more tricky. In the end, they found a small pile of burned-out tyres in front of a patch of scrubland, and they hid the axe there. 'When we get separated,' Ben told Halima, 'we'll meet back here, OK?'

And then they sprinted back through the village, towards the mine.

The rainfall had done a little to ease the humidity, but nothing to reduce the terrible heat of the day. As he ran, Ben felt his wet clothes steaming and becoming hot from the sunshine, the water boiling against his skin. He did his best to put the scorching sensation from his mind and tried to focus on the task ahead. It was a foolhardy venture, but it was the only thing they could think of.

Rather than take the main road up to the mine, Halima led them a more roundabout way that would keep them out of sight. It took them past the clearing where Ben had witnessed the dance to the ancestors a few nights previously, and through an area of forest that he would have found intimidating if he had not spent so much time in the jungle. They approached the mine from the south-east, and moved stealthily once they were away from the protection of the trees to avoid being seen by the occasional guard who was milling around with the standard AK-47. Before long, Suliman's office, with his old Land Rover still parked outside, was in sight.

The children caught their breath. 'Are you sure you're happy to do this?' Ben asked Halima, though the steely look of determination in her eyes told him he needn't have worried.

'Be at the meeting place as quickly as you can,' she told him, before flashing him a quick smile of encouragement. 'What is it you say?' She searched for the words. 'Break a leg?'

Ben nodded. 'Break a leg, Halima.'

And with that, the girl strode out into full view, marched towards Suliman's office and knocked firmly on the door.

Ben held his breath as he watched her jog a few metres back so as to put some distance between herself and the mine manager when he opened up. If the situation hadn't been so serious, the look on Suliman's face when he saw Halima would almost have been funny. Clearly he had never expected to see her again; clearly he thought that by now she was nothing more than a rotting or half-eaten corpse in the rainforest. He stared at her in astonishment for a few moments, allowing Halima time to turn and run, before calling out at his guards in Kikongo. Ben watched in satisfaction as his guards ran past the place where he was concealed, followed by Suliman as they chased Halima into the cover of the trees, barking instructions at her.

He just hoped Halima was fast enough to get away. She had done a great job of getting both Suliman and his guards out of his way, and now it was up to him to do his part.

The coast now clear, Ben made his move. He sprinted towards Suliman's office, and slipped inside. His eyes flickered over to the satellite phone, and he was tempted to make another attempt at calling; but that was going to have to wait. He didn't know how long he had, and it was imperative that he found the key to Suliman's battered Land Rover. Ben desperately started searching, upturning papers and opening drawers – it had to be here somewhere, but for the life of him he couldn't find it. Suddenly he smiled. He ran outside, opened the driver's door, and nodded in mute satisfaction.

The keys were still there, in the ignition.

Ben climbed in, took a deep breath, and started the engine.

He had never driven a car before. I've flown a microlight over the burning skies of Adelaide, though, he told himself. How hard can it be? He knew the principle – he just had to put it into practice.

The gearbox choked in protest as he tried to pump the vehicle into first gear. He pressed gingerly down on the accelerator, then lifted the clutch. It jumped forward, shaking Ben's body violently, then stalled.

Ben turned the key and tried again. This time he managed to get the Land Rover to move a few metres before it shuddered to a halt. He banged on the steering wheel in frustration. 'Come on!' he shouted, half to himself, half to the vehicle. Then, realizing that getting angry was not going to achieve anything, he took a deep breath to steady himself and tried again.

This time he managed to bring the clutch up slowly and without stalling. He started moving, and steered his way towards the road that led into the village, ignoring the screams of the engine that told him he was driving too fast for the low gear he was in. Ben didn't want to risk trying to change gear and stalling again – besides, he was fearful of going too quickly and having the vehicle veer out of control – so he stayed like this all the way into the village, concentrating furiously on steering the Land Rover around the huge potholes that littered his way as he bumped and jolted away from the mine.

He drew strange looks from the villagers as he headed through the central square. They knew it was Suliman's Land Rover – it was almost the only vehicle in the village, after all – and the sight of this young white boy driving it inexpertly through the streets, beeping his horn in panicked, staccato bursts whenever anybody got his way, was the most exciting thing many of them had seen for months. That Suliman would get to hear of it was inevitable, but Ben couldn't worry about that now. He had work to do.

Eventually the village and the villagers melted away as Ben approached the western outskirts of the city. In the distance, he could see the pile of rubber tyres where they had hidden the axe.

But there was no sign of Halima.

They were close behind her. Too close. As Halima ran through the trees, she could hear their voices and the crashing sound as they pounded after her. They were full-grown men with guns; she was a teenage girl. It was only a matter of time before she felt their strong hands on her – or their bullets in her shoulder blade. Her instinct was to hide, but if she did that, Ben would have to leave on his own, and she knew he needed her help. Besides, she didn't have time to find a good hiding place, and she couldn't be sure that they wouldn't find her. No, hiding wasn't an option. She had to go through with it. She had to succeed. And so, as she ran, she prayed to the ancestors that they would not catch her before she reached the rendezvous point.

Suddenly she tripped and fell crashing to the ground. She gasped in pain as she felt a sharpness rip through her twisted ankle. Lying there for a couple of seconds, stunned, she thought she might not be able to move. Something had torn badly at the bottom of her leg, and she knew that if she put pressure on it, it would be excruciating. Already she felt dizzy with the pain.

But the alternative was not an option. Suliman's men were closing in. They had already tried to kill her twice, and Halima had no intention of giving them a third chance. She pushed herself up with difficulty and tentatively put pressure on the damaged foot.

It was bad. Very bad. But she had to go on.

Limping desperately, she tried to run. It was difficult to move quickly – and agonizing – but she screwed up her face and tried to forget about the pain. Gradually she increased speed, but her limp stopped her from moving as fast as before. Her face was wet with sweat, and her mouth was dry.

'*La voilà!*' she heard one of the men shouting behind her. 'There she is!'

'Shoot her down!' another called.

Tears of pain were streaming down her cheeks now, and every step sent a tortuous flash up her wounded leg. But she didn't let up. She *couldn't* let up.

The road was not far now, she thought.

She hoped . . .

A million different possibilities flitted through Ben's brain. She had been caught; imprisoned; shot. Maybe now Suliman was forcing her, on pain of death, to tell him what she and Ben had been up to. It didn't bear thinking about.

He was by the tyres now, so he put his foot on the brake. The truck came to an abrupt and jolting stop, and Ben quickly climbed down and started scrabbling around in the undergrowth for the axe. It was there, but where was Halima?

Suddenly she burst through a nearby copse of trees. 'Hurry, Ben,' she shouted, her voice hoarse and weak but still urgent. 'They are behind me, they are close!'

Ben squinted his eyes. It looked like she was limping – certainly she wasn't running as quickly as he knew she could. He started moving towards her to help her, but she just screamed at him. 'No! The axe!'

He nodded briefly, spun round and yanked the axe up from the ground, then hurled it into the back of the Land Rover. By now, Halima was a few metres away, limping terribly, and he could see four armed men emerging from the trees behind her. 'Get in!' he yelled.

They both jumped up into the vehicle – Halima with the greatest difficulty. 'What happened?' Ben asked.

'It does not matter,' Halima told him through gritted teeth. 'I'll tell you later. Just move.' She clutched her leg as Ben turned his attention back to the Land Rover.

'Please don't stall,' he whispered to himself as he turned the key. The engine spluttered into life and he quickly knocked it into gear.

Crash! Halima screamed as her window shattered on the impact from a bullet, the glass showering into her arm. Ben felt a shard splinter into his forearm, but he couldn't waste time tending to it. The men were nearly upon them. He slammed his foot down on the accelerator and slowly raised the clutch. The Land Rover started to move.

Behind him he heard the sound of gunshot. He was going to have to increase the speed. The engine was emitting a high-pitched whine as the revs grew too high, and it refused to go any faster. 'Here goes,' Ben muttered. He slammed down the clutch and slipped into second gear, then brought his left foot up again. Success. He moved up into third gear, then fourth, and they zoomed down the road, leaving the sound of gunshots behind them and trying not to think about the dangers of landmines on the road. Abele had said they had done most of their killing, and he hoped he was right. He didn't want his first time behind the wheel to be his last.

Halima looked terrified as Ben tried to steer the speeding vehicle around the potholes in the road, and they were both thrown around by the bumpy surface. But Ben didn't dare slow down. They needed to get a good distance from the village if what they wanted to do was going to work.

And they needed to get there quickly.

CHAPTER TWENTY

Suliman's men had run after the Land Rover, but when it became clear that they weren't going to catch it they slowed down and regrouped. Just then, Suliman himself burst out from the trees. 'Where are they?' he screeched in Kikongo as he ran towards them. 'What have you done with them?'

The men – there were five of them – looked embarrassed as their boss approached. 'You!' Suliman pointed at one of them. 'What happened?'

The man looked nervously to his comrades. 'She got away,' he mumbled finally.

Suliman's eyes narrowed. 'What do you mean, she got away? Are you trying to tell me that a *girl* got the better of you?'

'The boy was waiting for her,' the man stuttered.

'They had your Land Rover . . .'

'My Land Rover?' Suliman spat. 'What were they doing with my Land Rover?'

But no one answered. They knew Suliman's moods, and they recognized the dangerous look in his eyes. He stared each one down in turn before settling his eyes finally on the man he had been speaking to.

'You,' he said to him. 'You speak too much.'

'Sorry, boss,' the man replied.

'Oh, you *will* be sorry,' Suliman whispered, before looking around again at the others. 'You will all be sorry.' With a serious frown, he addressed the man standing next to the one he had been picking on. 'You,' he said. 'Kill him.'

The man blinked at him in surprise. 'But boss, he's—'

'Don't argue with me!' Suliman shouted, his eyes bright with an awful fire. 'Kill him now.'

The man looked at his new prey, who was staggering backwards with a look of untold terror on his face, shaking his head and whispering, 'No, please.'

'Do it,' Suliman barked.

The man glanced uncomfortably around at the others, then raised his Kalashnikov. His prey screamed once, then turned and ran back towards the forest.

Bang!

The bullet hit him squarely in the middle of his

back and he fell to the ground. One of the men ran towards him to see if he was dead or just wounded, but Suliman called him back with a bark. 'Leave him!' Then he stared ferociously at the others. 'I don't want any more failures,' he said.

There was a horrible silence, then the man who had been forced to kill his friend spoke. 'But boss, how are we going to get them? They have taken the only vehicle left in the village.'

Suliman smiled a dead smile. 'No they haven't,' he said. 'Come with me.'

He turned and started jogging back into the village, his men following nervously behind.

They were perhaps seven or eight miles out of the village – Ben couldn't tell for sure as he had been concentrating so hard on just keeping the Land Rover on the road – when they came to a halt. The forest on either side of the road was very dense – it would be impossible to drive any vehicle off the road and round any obstruction – and this particular stretch of road was long and straight; from where they had stopped, they would be able to see people coming – in either direction.

'This'll do,' Ben said, pointing just ahead of them and to the side of the road. If they could block the road just here, there would be no way anyone could reach Udok by car and it would be a long walk with the dangers of the jungle either side; if Ben could get his message through to Sam Garner again, perhaps they would have gained the time they needed to seal the village before anyone else could get in and be infected. And, of course, no one could now leave by this road and take the virus out of Udok either. He hoped.

The two of them opened their doors simultaneously and climbed down. Halima was clearly in great pain, but she said nothing about it. Wordlessly Ben took the axe from the back of the truck and headed to the side of the road.

He had his eye on a tall tree – tall enough, he estimated, to cover the width of the road once he had felled it. It was not as thick as some of the trees around, but it was thick enough – if he was going to hack it down, it would take some work. Ben raised the axe over his right shoulder and brought it down with all his force onto the side of the trunk that was furthest away from the road. The blade stuck into the bark and he had to give it a mighty yank to pull it back out again. The second swipe entered the tree several centimetres higher than the first cut. Ben's brow furrowed – this was going to be more difficult than he had imagined.

Meanwhile Halima was in the road, keeping watch.

Their plan was to cut down the tree to stop any bus-load of workers being able to gain passage to the village; and they needed to have as much advance warning as possible if Suliman and his men were following. They didn't *think* there was another vehicle still in the village for them to use; but they weren't sure.

Ben kept hacking away. The sun was high and hot, casting short shadows on the ground; before long, sweat was dripping down his face into his eyes, and the handle of the axe was slipping in his perspiring palms. He felt his muscles burning with the exertion, and it was all he could do to keep going. But he gritted his teeth and thought of his father, bleeding and weak on that bed. If he didn't stop this busload of people from arriving in Udok, they would meet the same fate.

He was a third of the way through the trunk now. He continued cutting the tree, the occasional grunt of exertion the only sound punctuating the silence between him and the ever-observant Halima.

Suddenly she shouted, 'There is someone coming!'

Ben stopped, automatically looking back towards the village to see if Suliman was upon them. But there was nothing coming from that direction. With a sick feeling he turned round. Sure enough, indistinct because of the heat haze but definitely there nonetheless, he could see a minibus. It was impossible to say how far away it was, or how quickly it was travelling, but Ben didn't allow himself the time to stop and watch it, instead running back to the tree and redoubling his efforts with the axe.

'Hurry, Ben!' he heard Halima shout, panic in her voice. 'They are nearly here!'

Ben slammed the axe into the tree with as much force as he could muster; when he tried to pull it out, though, it would not come, no matter how much he tweaked and jiggled it. 'Come here, Halima!' he yelled.

She limped to his side, her black face strangely pale. 'What do you want me to do?'

'Push!'

There was no way, Ben realized, that he was going to cut all the way through the tree trunk before the minibus had passed them; their only hope was to pray that he had cut deeply enough into the trunk to be able to push it over and let the weight of the tree itself do the rest of the work. They placed their hands against the bark and started to take the strain.

There was a slight groan from the tree, but it only wavered fractionally. 'Again,' Ben shouted. 'One, two, three, push!'

Halima cried out a little as she put all her force behind it. This time there was more movement, and the sound of cracking from inside the wound Ben had inflicted on the trunk with his axe.

But now he could also hear the sound of the minibus, the rattly growl of its diesel engine growing nearer and nearer. They pushed again, and again. The trunk creaked and cracked, then finally – with a massive tearing noise – it toppled and fell over, landing with a heavy thump across the road. Ben heard the sudden squeak of brakes, and the two of them ran back into the middle of the road. The minibus had stopped about fifteen metres beyond where the tree had fallen, and the driver was climbing down, waving his arms at the children and shouting abuse at them in Kikongo. Then he was pushed to one side as two burly men jumped out. They took one look at Ben and Halima and started bounding towards them.

'Get in the Land Rover,' Ben shrieked. 'We can't let them get near to us, we might infect them.' But Halima was already halfway there. He clambered in and fumbled for the keys in the ignition. The men were jumping over the tree trunk by the time the engine coughed into action. He slammed the gear stick into reverse and moved backwards as quickly as he could. Yet again the engine started screaming as he hit top speed for the low reverse gear, and the men were gaining on him. Ben needed to speed up, but to do that he had to be facing in the opposite direction.

'Hold on,' he told Halima. 'I'm going to turn.'

Halima nodded and clutched the sides of her seat firmly. Ben took a deep breath and spun the wheel round quickly to the right. The tyres skidded noisily as the vehicle moved round through a hundred and eighty degrees before coming to a jolting stop. Ben knocked it into first gear again, then breathlessly moved away. In his wing mirrors he noted, with satisfaction, that his pursuers had stopped and were arguing angrily with each other as the Land Rover sped back towards the village.

They drove in silence as the road started curving round and the scene of chaos they had caused behind them disappeared from view. But they couldn't stay silent for ever. 'What are we going to do now?' Halima asked.

'I don't know for sure,' Ben replied. 'I think we should try and get back to Suliman's office, see if we can make that phone call again. All we've done here is buy ourselves some time but—'

He stopped in mid-sentence and slammed his foot on the brakes. Because there, in front of them, parked sideways across the road, was a car. The same car Ben, Charles and Abele had taken from the bandit the day they had arrived in Udok. Surrounding it were a group of armed men – Ben was too shocked to count how many – and at their head was the unmistakable tall, lanky figure of Suliman.

Ben's eyes narrowed as the man stared at him, a nasty sneer on his face.

Time seemed to stand still.

'Listen carefully,' Ben breathed, trying to stop his lips from moving. 'I think there's enough space for me to get round the side of the car. I'm going to drive straight at it until the last minute, then turn. As soon as we start moving, duck down out of sight, because they'll probably start firing. OK?'

'What about you, Ben?'

'I'm going to have to take my chances. Ready?'

'Ready.'

'One, two, *three*.' Ben slammed the accelerator down and headed straight for the men in front of him. But rather than scramble, as he had expected them to, they stood their ground. They aimed their AK-47s at the Land Rover, some of them pointing at the wheels, others at the windscreen.

And then they fired.

The windscreen turned opaque on the first impact of the bullets, blinding Ben's view momentarily before the glass shattered all over him. But even if he had been able to see properly, it wouldn't have done any good, because the two front tyres had been ripped apart by the bullets. Ben felt the vehicle veer dangerously, and even if he hadn't felt the need to duck away from the next onslaught of enemy fire, he would not have been able to keep the Land Rover under control. It swerved to the side of the road and came to a thumping and devastating stop as it smashed into a tree.

Within seconds, the men were upon them, dragging Ben and Halima roughly from the front seats and hurling them onto the ground in front of Suliman.

Ben looked up at his nemesis. There was a band of sweat beads forming on his upper lip and he looked immensely pleased with himself. He bent down and whispered, his mouth so close to Ben's ear that he could feel the sticky hotness of his breath. 'You have caused me much trouble, Ben Tracey,' he said.

Ben turned his face so that he was looking straight into Suliman's eyes. 'You're not going to get away with this.'

'Of course I am, you idiot. You two will be dead in less than a minute. Your fool of a father no doubt already is. And I hope you don't think that that peasant Abele will help you – last time I saw him, he was dying in ditch on the side of the road. You should have stayed in England, instead of trying to interfere with things you do not understand.'

Halima spoke. 'It's you who don't understand—'

'Silence!' Suliman said sharply. 'You are the most foolish of all, getting involved with these white men.'

He stood up and took a few steps back.

'The last time I ordered your execution,' he said, 'you were very lucky to get away. This time . . .' He shook his head meaningfully, then nodded at another of his men.

He approached with his rifle.

Ben started to shake as blind fear grabbed hold of him; he felt icy cold, as though all the strength that remained in his body had suddenly ebbed away, and he could tell that Halima was experiencing the same thing. He had to do something. Say something. Persuade Suliman that he was doing the wrong thing. But his mind wouldn't think straight, and in his dreadful state of panic there seemed to be an incessant buzzing in his ears that would not allow him to concentrate.

'What about the ancestors?' he heard himself shouting to Suliman, but his captor didn't seem moved by the threat.

The buzzing in Ben's ears grew louder; it was only with difficulty that he heard Suliman's next order. 'Kill them,' he shouted.

Suliman's man stepped towards them, rifle in his hand. His face was fixed into an unpleasant grin and he waved the gun between Ben and Halima as though teasing them with the threat of his imminent violence. The two of them stepped backwards towards the side of the road, Ben holding Halima steady as he could tell that her injured leg was making it difficult to walk, trying to get into the shelter of the forest but unwilling to turn their backs on this grinning assassin. Out of the corner of his eye, Ben could see Suliman cast his head over his shoulder nervously, as though he was aware of something approaching and wanted his business over and done with so he could get out of there. 'Do it!' he screamed.

The man raised his gun and aimed it at Ben's head. He was about ten metres away, and his trigger finger was twitching. As they stepped backwards again, Ben and Halima tripped over a branch and fell heavily to the ground. The assassin's smile grew broader. He lowered his aim and took another step forward towards the side of the road.

Nobody heard the click of the hidden landmine as he trod on it; but the explosion was so loud that for one deathly moment Ben thought he had been shot. The devastating effect of the landmine on the assassin soon put that thought from his mind. He was thrown two metres in the air and landed awkwardly in a scrambled heap somewhere between the exploded landmine and where Ben and Halima were sitting.

The leg that had stepped onto the firing mechanism appeared to have been splintered in two along its length and blood was pouring out of the wound. His other limbs were gnarled and disjointed from the way he had fallen and his face was covered in blood and dirt. For a few horrible seconds his body twitched in the dust and then it lay still.

Everyone around looked at the dead man in shock; when he managed to snap out of it, Ben fully expected Suliman to order another of his men to kill them, and he prepared to lift Halima from the ground and run. But Suliman's attention had been diverted: he was looking all around and up into the sky, clearly worried, and Ben realized that the buzzing sound had not just been in his ears – everyone could hear it, and it was getting louder. It was more of a roar now, and all the guards – including the one Suliman had instructed to shoot them – were looking up to the sky.

Then they saw them.

Hovering into view above the trees came two khaki-coloured Chinook helicopters. Their double rotary blades whipped up a deafening roar and caused the branches of the trees to blow back as if they were in the path of a gale. Ben felt the hair on his head being blown around, but his attention was fixed on Suliman and his men. They were staggering backwards, buffeted by the winds and looking scared and confused. They were not going to be carrying out Suliman's order. Not yet.

And then there was a voice, coming out over a loudspeaker from one of the Chinooks. It spoke in French first. '*Ici la force de maintien de la paix de l'ONU. Déposez vos armes. Je répète, déposez vos armes.*'

Ben looked desperately around him, unable to understand what was going on. And then he almost crumpled with relief as the voice spoke in English.

'This is the United Nations peacekeeping force,' it called. 'Throw down your weapons. I repeat, throw down your weapons.'

CHAPTER TWENTY-ONE

Suddenly there was confusion all around. The choppers manoeuvred themselves so that everyone was closed in and unable to escape either way down the road, and as they hovered, trap doors opened in the bottom and ropes dangled down. Almost before Ben knew what was happening, he saw figures in protective white suits being winched down. They looked terrifying, their faces masked with complicated breathing apparatus and their bodies encased in sealed clothing – like something out of a science-fiction movie, Ben thought. They carried guns, too, and as soon as they were on the ground they started rounding everybody up, indiscriminately, pointing their weapons in such a way that made it quite clear they would not hesitate to use them.

'What is happening?' Halima screamed desperately over the noise of the Chinooks' propellers.

'I don't know,' Ben shouted back.

Suliman was shouting too, barking instructions at his men that Ben couldn't make out; but the sight of the peacekeepers had thrown them into a frenzy of panic, and they were at that very moment throwing down their weapons. When Suliman realized what was happening, however, his eyes narrowed and he quietened down.

Whenever Ben tried to remember what took place next, he always found himself confused by a jumble of memories. He saw Suliman talking earnestly to one of the masked men, while the Chinooks landed in the road and the faceless, uniformed men ordered them all – in voices that sounded strangely robotic through the breathing apparatus – to make their way into the choppers.

And then they were sitting on the hard, un-comfortable floor with Suliman and his men looking on at them with pure hatred. Suliman particularly refused to take his dead eyes off Ben, who could only imagine what was going through his head. Only the threatening presence of three peacekeeping guards and their weapons stopped the situation erupting into violence – of that, Ben was sure. The guys from the UN might look scary, he thought to himself, but he was glad they were there.

Clearly Sam Garner must have heard his message.

'Where are we going?' he shouted at the guard who was nearest them as he felt the Chinook rise up into the air.

'Back to the village you came from, sir,' came the reply in a Midwestern American accent.

'Then what?'

There was a pause. 'Quarantine.'

Ben nodded grimly. Deep down it was what he had expected, but that didn't make it any easier to hear.

'Are there doctors arriving?' he asked. 'With medicine?' He was desperate to know what sort of chance his dad had.

The guard nodded. 'They're on their way. But from what I've seen . . .' His voice trailed off, and Ben could not persuade him to continue.

It only took a couple of minutes to fly back to the village, and the scene appeared to Ben to be one of organized mayhem. Chinooks seemed to be flying in from all around, and the place was swarming with masked, white-suited men unloading equipment and barking instructions at the frightened-looking villagers who were being herded around into small groups. Signs with the words '*Cordon Sanitaire*' had been put up all over the place; tents and a few more solid-looking structures were being erected with surprising speed.

Ben watched in horror as he saw stretcher after stretcher of the ill and the dying being carried into one of those tents. A long, canvas-covered corridor led out the back of it to an area Ben couldn't see. 'Where does that lead?' he asked the guard who had brusquely helped him and Halima down from the chopper.

'You don't want to know,' came the terse reply.

'I *do* want to know,' Ben shouted at him, his patience wearing thin. 'I'm the one who raised the alarm. I'm the one who got you here. Where does it go?'

The guard seemed to consider that for a moment. Finally he answered. 'Incinerator,' he said. 'They're building it now. We can't risk just burying the bodies.'

Ben let that sink in. 'I need to speak to the person in charge.'

The guard shook his head. 'We have our orders, sir. You need to proceed to the processing area.'

'No,' Ben argued. 'You don't understand. There are people in Kinshasa who knew—'

'The processing area, sir,' the guard said firmly, taking a firmer grip on his rifle.

Ben wasn't going to be bullied. Not now. 'You're either going to let me speak to whoever's in charge, or you're going to have to shoot me.' He jutted his chin out.

The guard appeared to think about it. Eventually he took a radio handset from his belt and spoke into it.

'This is Alpha Nine. I've got the English kid here. He's insisting on speaking to the commander. Over.'

There was a short crackle, and then another voice came over the radio. 'Roger that.'

Thirty seconds later, another masked man approached. 'What's the problem here?'

The guard started to speak, but Ben interrupted him. 'My name's Ben Tracey. I'm the person who informed Dr Sam Garner about the virus, and I'm the person who has just stopped a busload of people from the next village from entering Udok – so please stop fobbing me off.'

'OK, Ben,' the masked man said in a pacifying tone of voice. 'You need to calm down – I know who you are. What can I do for you?'

'Tell me what's happening for a start.'

'We're sealing the village. Everyone who may have come into contact with the virus is being placed into quarantine.' He paused. 'We were warned that you would be here, Ben, but I'm afraid my orders are very explicit. There can be no exceptions.'

'I know that,' said Ben urgently. 'But you have to listen to me. I know things about the virus – information that you have to have. I know where the virus is coming from.'

'OK, son. You'd better tell me what you've got.'

'It's the mine. You've got to seal it. My dad's a

scientist and he thinks the reservoir – that's the organism that's harbouring the virus – is down there. It started off just killing bats in the cave, but now it's killing humans. There's no point simply sealing the village – you've got to make sure nobody else ever goes down there and that the infected bats don't fly out.'

Ben couldn't tell if the masked man had taken anything on board. 'Is there anything else,' he simply asked in his American drawl.

'Yes,' Ben stated fiercely. He pointed in the direction of where Suliman was walking to the processing area. 'When you picked us up, that man was trying to kill us, and he's been trying to kill us pretty much since we arrived. He knew about the virus, and he knew I might alert people. Put us in quarantine if you have to, but keep us away from him. He's a psycho.'

'What do you mean, he knew about the virus? Why would he put himself in danger like that? From what I can tell, everyone here thinks it's down to some sort of supernatural mumbo-jumbo.'

'Not Suliman,' Ben insisted. 'You have to believe me.'

'Excuse me, sir,' the guard who had accompanied them in the chopper interrupted.

'Go ahead, soldier.'

'It's true that the men we just picked up were

armed, but they claim it was because the kids stole a
Land Rover that they were trying to get back.'

The boss looked back to Ben and Halima. 'This
true, son?'

'Yes,' Ben said with a sinking feeling, 'but—'

'I don't blame you trying to escape the village, son,
but that's not going to happen now.'

'I wasn't trying to escape the village!' Ben shouted.
'I was—'

'OK, I've heard enough,' the commander overruled
him. 'Our directions are clear: everyone's to be kept in
quarantine. Nobody in there will be armed, so you
should be perfectly safe.' He turned and walked away,
leaving the guard to push Ben and Halima in the
direction of a small group of villagers who were being
organized by another of the faceless peacekeepers.

'Just shut down the mine!' Ben shouted over his
shoulder. 'Whatever you do, shut down the mine!'

Seething with frustration, they started trudging to
where the man had indicated. But Ben was hardly
concentrating on where he was going, his attention
diverted by the sight of more sick people being
stretchered into the canvas tent. He knew perfectly
well what he was looking for.

A white face.

He was halfway to the processing area when he saw
it. Instantly he ran towards his father, doing his best

to keep tears from welling up in his eyes; but before he had run even a few metres, he heard shouts from all around him. Appearing as if from nowhere, two armed peacekeepers stood between Ben and his dad. 'Stand back!' they shouted.

'No,' Ben snapped at them. 'It's OK, it's my dad.'

'No cross-contamination,' the peacekeeper insisted in an emotionless American accent. 'If you do not stand down, I *will* be forced to shoot. There will *not* be a second warning.'

Ben stood still. All eyes seemed to be on him. He looked past the guards to where his dad was being carried. Russell Tracey's face was still and pale; Ben watched in desperation as he was carried into the tent. Then he looked back at the peacekeepers, who still had their assault rifles aimed at him. Reluctantly he turned and trudged back to Halima.

'Maybe he is all right,' Halima said without much conviction. Ben didn't reply.

Ahead of them was a disturbance. Ben saw without surprise that Suliman was arguing with someone giving him instructions. Immediately he too was surrounded by two more armed peacekeepers, and eventually he moved, with a surly look but without further complaint, towards a group of people milling around waiting for yet more instructions.

As Ben and Halima approached, they realized that

males and females were being separated. Distraught and tearful mothers were being forcibly removed from their sons; and fathers of daughters stood alone and confused as their families were taken away from them. Ben felt a sudden pang. He had been with Halima non-stop for days now; they had gone through such a lot together. Now he was to be separated not only from his father but also from the one person who had helped him through all this. He didn't want to leave her.

They stopped walking and turned to look at each other. 'We have to keep telling them to shut the mine,' Ben said quietly.

'I know,' Halima replied.

There was an awkward stillness between them, as they both searched for the right words to say. 'You will be all right,' Halima managed finally.

Ben tried to wear a brave smile. 'Hope so. Look, they can't keep us separated for ever. I'll probably see you before—'

But Halima had put a finger gently to his lips. 'You have done all that you need to do here, Ben. But you do not belong in this place. Promise me you will persuade them to let you go home as soon as possible.'

He looked into her eyes. 'I'll see you before then.' He glanced towards the medical tent. 'If I'm OK, I mean.'

Halima smiled. 'Perhaps. Perhaps not.' Her gaze lingered. 'But I will not forget you, Ben Tracey, or what you have done.'

And with that, she turned and joined the other women, not looking back to see Ben watching her leave, his face expressionless and his jaw clenched.

He took a deep breath to steady his raging emotions, then stepped towards the male villagers.

The rest of the day passed in a blur. Ignored by the African men around him, Ben followed as they were led into yet another tent. There they were instructed to remove their clothes. Ben did as he was told, standing awkwardly with the other naked, skinny, bedraggled men while their clothes were taken to the incinerator – in fact more of a huge bonfire – to be burned. They were then led outside again where plastic bottles full of stinking disinfectant were poured over their heads. When it dried, they were handed clean clothes – simple cloth trousers and T-shirts that made them look more like a group of convicts than anything else.

They then lined up to have their blood tested. The men ahead of Ben looked deeply scared as they waited for the American doctor – also masked and suited – to slide the slim, sharp needle into their veins. Many of them looked like they wanted to run, but they could not do so as they were being held at gunpoint.

Eventually it was Ben's turn. The doctor looked at his white skin in surprise. 'You OK, pal?' he asked through his mask.

Ben shrugged. 'Kind of.' The doctor started dabbing an antiseptic wipe on his arm. 'Have they shut the mine down yet? It's really important.'

'Not my area.' He picked up a needle. 'You must be the guy that alerted us to the virus.'

'Yeah.' Half of Ben wanted to go into detail, but he was overcome with exhaustion now. He winced as the sharp needle punctured his skin. His blood slowly filled the syringe. 'What's the blood test for?' he asked.

'Antibodies,' the doctor explained. 'Some people are immune to viruses like this – that's why not everyone has fallen ill. I'm afraid you won't be able to leave the quarantine area until we've been able to confirm that you're not a carrier.'

Or that I am, Ben thought to himself. 'How long will that take?'

'Couple of days. The samples have to be flown back to the lab in Kinshasa.'

'But I've been in contact with it and I haven't got ill. Surely that proves—'

'Don't prove a thing, son. These things can take up to twenty days to become symptomatic.'

Twenty days. Ben felt a sickness in his stomach.

'And what if I'm not immune?'

The doctor hesitated before asking. 'Then I'm afraid you're going to have to stay in the village until the virus has run its course.'

Ben nodded gravely, before he asked the question that had been on his mind ever since he arrived back at the village. 'Um, you know the big tent – the one leading to the incinerator?'

The doctor nodded.

'The people they take there, are they all going to die?'

Again a pause. 'Most of them, son,' he replied. 'We're giving everyone antipyretics to reduce their body temperatures and antibiotics to deal with the virus, although it's too early for us to say whether they will have any effect. My own opinion is that they probably won't. In the end it'll come down to chance. A few people will make it, but it's impossible to say who.'

Ben went quiet.

'What's the matter, son?' the doctor asked quietly. 'Someone you know in there?'

'Yeah,' Ben replied. 'Yeah, you could say that.'

He walked away from the doctor and followed the line of people to a nearby tent. A sign outside said in big letters '*Quarantaine Masculine*'. Male quarantine.

He took a deep breath, and walked inside.

CHAPTER TWENTY-TWO

The first few hours in quarantine were the worst.

Ben had only been in the tent for a very short while when, beyond the hubbub of frightened voices, he started hearing distant screams. At first he thought that they were human, but soon he realized that the sounds were too high-pitched for that, and too herd-like. In an instant he realized what it was. The village's livestock – the mangy cows and goats that he had seen wandering around – would be an infection risk. They had to be slaughtered. Ben couldn't work out if what he was hearing was the sound of animals having their throats cut, or their squeals of terror as they witnessed what was happening to their fellow beasts. Either way, it curdled his blood.

But it had to be endured. Now that there was

nothing for Ben to do but sit and wait, his mind started working overtime. What if he had the virus? What if he was only a few days away from death? He wanted to think that he was brave enough to put up with the agony those who fell ill with this awful disease went through; brave enough to face up to it like his dad had; but he couldn't be sure that he was.

He was just going to have to wait. Wait for the result of the test, or the telltale signs that the virus was taking hold of him. It was like some awful game of Russian roulette, only someone else was pulling the trigger. He felt horribly alone.

They had not been in the area for long when a pungent, stomach-churning smell hit their noses. The villagers all started talking to each other in frightened whispers, but Ben couldn't understand what they were saying. He didn't need to, though. Somehow, without knowing how he knew, he realized that the stench that had filled the village was that of burning flesh. The incinerator had begun its grisly work, and the smell did not let up. It seemed there were plenty of dead bodies to feed the fire.

Although he could not understand the villagers, he could tell that they were confused and frightened, and he understood why. They had never seen a television programme or a magazine. They had no idea who these masked intruders were, or why they were doing these things to them. There were advantages, though, to not speaking English. Ben realized that shortly after the smell of the incinerators hit him and he overheard the guards talking.

'It's started,' one of them said grimly.

'Yeah,' one of them agreed. 'Just thank your lucky stars you're not on grave detail.'

When Ben heard that, he stared at them in horror, remembering the sight of the mass grave outside the village. Of course, the bodies there would have to be incinerated too. What would these poor people think when they realized what was going on, that their dead relatives were being exhumed and cremated without ceremony? What would Halima think? Her parents were there.

And what would she say about the ancestors . . . ?

Then there was another sound – a huge explosion this time that shocked everyone in the tent into silence. When he heard it, Ben jumped to his feet. He was not the only one; once the villagers had shaken off the momentary shock, many of them also stood up and started shouting – scared, no doubt, that something was happening to their families and homes. Sensing a potential riot, the guards started waving their guns towards them, shouting at them to sit down. Gradually the panic subsided; but then there was another loud bang.

This time, Ben pushed through the crowd. 'What's going on?' he asked one of the guards.

'Nothing for you to worry about, sir.'

'There's *plenty* for me to be worried about,' Ben shouted. 'What's going on.'

'Dynamite explosions,' the guard told him.

'Where?'

'The mine. They're closing it up. Making sure nothing can get in or out.' Suddenly he pushed past Ben. 'Everyone sit down!' he yelled. '*Asseyez-vous! Tout de suite!*'

But Ben hardly heard the instructions he was giving the villagers. For the first time in a long while he had allowed a grin to spread across his face.

The mine was shut.

The virus was contained.

They had done it.

It did not take long for the smile to fall from his face, however. As he turned round, his eyes immediately settled on Suliman, who was gazing at him implacably from the other side of the tent. Suliman had not appeared distraught at the sound of the explosions; it was clear that he knew what was going on.

He remained calm; he spoke to nobody; he just kept his eyes on Ben, his gaze steady. He looked for all the world like he was waiting for something.

Waiting for his chance.

Ben stayed close to the UN guards, unsure what Suliman was planning, but certain that he was planning something. Suliman realized that Ben knew what he – and his bosses – had been up to. One word from him to the right person could incriminate them all. Ben knew what Suliman was capable of; he knew that Suliman would do whatever it took to silence him.

Time passed, and Ben grew increasingly nervous. The strain of waiting for Suliman to make his move became increasingly hard to bear in that hot, crowded, terrifying place. Eventually he couldn't stand it any more. He stood up and approached one of the guards who were standing at the entrance to the quarantine tent. 'I need to get out of here,' he said quietly.

The guard shook his masked head. 'No one leaves,' he stated sternly.

'Look, you don't understand. I'm not safe here. That man . . .'

'*No one leaves*,' the guard repeated. He was joined by his colleague, and they both clutched their rifles. Ben looked at them in desperate frustration before furiously turning his back on them and going back to find his place.

The hours ticked slowly by. As darkness fell, the tent became quieter, but somehow Ben knew Suliman was not asleep. He did his best to stay awake, but as the night passed, his body became overcome with exhaustion, and no matter how many times he told himself to remain wary, his heavy eyelids soon started to flutter and close.

It happened just before morning. Ben, along with everyone else in the quarantine camp, had been drowsing, and the UN guards on duty were standing outside of the entrance to the tent. Suddenly Ben was awakened by a fist across his mouth and his neck in a deadlock. 'Make one noise,' Suliman's voice said, 'and I will break your neck.'

Ben's eyes shot open and he struggled to breathe.

'Stand up very slowly.' Suliman's voice was snake-like. Ben did as he was told. In the darkness, he became aware of someone else by his side – one of Suliman's accomplices. He could also tell that a few people around him were awake; they could sense that something was happening, but they weren't going to get involved. Suliman pushed Ben to the side of the tent, his grip round the boy's neck deathly tight, while his man ripped the bottom of the canvas up to create an exit.

Within seconds they were outside. Suliman spoke to his accomplice in Kikongo and the man slipped back into the tent to keep a lookout as Ben was marched swiftly and silently away.

They stopped. Ben was feeling light-headed and was unsure exactly where they were, but Suliman appeared to have been able to dodge the peacekeepers in the relative stillness of the night. He didn't speak. He just started to tighten his grip.

Ben tried to shout out, but the only noise that came was a choking sound from his throat. His arms flailed in the air as he tried to struggle away from his attacker, but Suliman kept his grip tight and hard, and gradually Ben's movements started to suffer for lack of oxygen. His efforts became weaker and weaker; everything started to spin; his limbs became powerless.

And then, as though in a dream, Ben saw someone approach from the darkness. His gait was stumbling, his expression more dead than alive. But even in his state of strangulated semi-consciousness, he recognized the figure that was drawing nearer.

It was Abele.

The expression on his face told of the effort of every move. Painfully, his breath rasping, he bent down and picked a jagged stone about the size of a grapefruit from the ground. He staggered towards the struggling pair and with what strength he had left in his arms brought the stone firmly down on the top of Suliman's head.

The mine manager roared with pain, but did not let

Ben go; so Abele struck him a second time. This time his grip loosened, and Ben – drawing great gulps of air into his protesting lungs – managed to get away. Now Suliman was upon Abele, who stood no chance against a man with his full strength at his disposal. In an instant, Abele was on the ground; Suliman had taken his stone from him and was preparing to pummel it into his head.

'Stop!'

The UN guards had been alerted by Suliman's roar, and suddenly there were several of them – Ben couldn't count how many in all the confusion – guns at the ready. Suliman's arm stopped in mid-air as he caught sight of the peacekeepers, but his face was a picture of indecision and fury.

'Drop it!' one of the masked figures shouted.

It all happened in a split second. There was a wildness in Suliman's eyes that suggested his anger had taken hold of what good sense he had; with a hiss he started to bring the stone down towards Abele's head.

It only took one shot.

The bullet from the peacekeeper's rifle was aimed to kill and it entered Suliman's skull right in the middle of his forehead. The mine manager was thrown down to the floor with a thud, and in the bright moonlight Ben could see the blood dripping from his head into a sticky puddle. There were a few seconds of horrified silence, during which time Suliman's right foot twitched alarmingly; but it was clear to everyone watching that he was quite dead.

Ben's instinct was to run to Abele, to see if he was OK. But as he tried to do so, he felt himself being restrained from behind. 'Get a stretcher here,' an American voice called from somewhere. Within moments, Abele was being lifted onto a stretcher and carried towards the hospital tent.

'You're going to be OK, Abele,' Ben shouted, his voice wavering. But he didn't know if that was true. And of course, Abele didn't reply. Ben listened as his noisy breathing disappeared into the night, before he was led silently back to the quarantine area, his body shaking with the brutal horror of what had just happened.

The doctor had told Ben he would be in the quarantine tent for two days before he received the result of his test. In the event, it was three.

It was gruelling. Every couple of hours, someone would start displaying the signs of the virus; they would instantly be removed by the faceless medics and taken, often shouting and screaming, to the medical tents. Word had got round now that few who entered that place would return, and the constant acrid smell from the incinerators served as an ever-present reminder of what would happen to them. Ben felt like he was in some kind of concentration camp, waiting for the inevitable call, and he started to share the increasing panic that the occupants of the tent were experiencing. Arguments began to break out as the villagers demanded to know what was going on; occasionally the guys from the UN had to settle them by force, which did nothing to ease anyone's fears.

On the second day – when Ben was just thinking to himself that he never wanted to see another bowl of the mashed cassava root that was given to them from a huge cauldron three times a day – the guards were approached by two more masked UN men. They spoke briefly and Ben watched as one of the guards pointed in his direction. The masked men started walking towards him and he stood up to receive them.

'Hi, Ben,' one of them said. Clearly they had spoken before, but the fact that these people were all wearing masks meant that one American accent merged into another for him. He nodded. 'Ben,' the man continued. 'I'm afraid I have bad news for you.'

Ben closed his eyes as a sudden hotness ran through his veins.

'The man called Abele. He was a friend of yours, I understand.'

Ben nodded again. 'Kind of,' he said, his voice clipped

so that it didn't reveal the emotion he was feeling.

'I'm sorry, Ben. He died about an hour ago. He was too far gone – there was nothing anyone could do.'

Ben took a deep breath. 'Thank you for telling me,' he whispered, doing his best to keep his wavering voice steady. 'Do you have any information about my father?'

There was an ominous pause. 'I'm sorry, Ben. No. It's too early to tell.'

Ben nodded, then turned and walked to the edge of the tent. He desperately wanted to be alone but, since that was not possible, he wanted to get away from anybody who could speak to him in his own language. From the corner of his eye he watched the UN men leave.

He could not get the image of poor Abele that first time they had met at Kinshasa Airport out of his head. Ben had been suspicious of him then – how wrong could he have been? And if Abele had been beaten by this terrible disease – strong, unbeatable Abele – what chance did anyone have? What chance did his dad have? What chance did Ben himself have? His emotions a cocktail of mourning and fear, he collapsed to the ground with his head in his hands. It was down to fate now. All he could do was wait. Now that he knew Abele was dead, the smell of the incinerators seemed ten times worse.

The results arrived the following day.

A masked man carrying a large clipboard entered the tent. He had an air of authority and everyone fell silent as he started reading names out, his American accent struggling with the unfamiliar African sounds. One by one, the villagers stood up and walked to him, terrified apprehension in their eyes. He said something to them that Ben couldn't hear and they were sent outside.

He found himself holding his breath as he waited for his name.

Finally it came. 'Ben Tracey,' the announcer called. Ben stood up and slowly walked towards him.

'Leave the tent and bear to the left.'

'What's my test result?' Ben asked directly.

'Leave the tent and bear to the left.' The faceless man simply repeated his instruction.

Ben nodded curtly, gritted his teeth and stepped outside, accompanied by another UN guard. 'This way,' his companion told him.

He walked over to where a small group of Africans were standing with worried, uncomprehending looks on their faces. Every now and then, someone else would join them; but they were few and far between – most of the villagers were sent elsewhere. Where it was, Ben couldn't see.

Finally the man holding the clipboard approached. He walked straight up to Ben.

'Ben Tracey?'

Ben nodded. He didn't trust himself to speak.

'I'm giving you the news first,' he said flatly. 'The others will have to wait for an interpreter.'

'OK.'

'Samples have been taken from those infected with the virus so that we can isolate the specific antibody that fights it. You have been tested for that antibody.'

Ben wished the man wasn't wearing a mask – that way he might have been able to read something into his expression. But he couldn't.

'Only about one third of the population carry this antibody,' he continued. 'I'm happy to inform you that you are one of those.'

Ben felt his knees buckle beneath him with relief; it was all he could do to stand up straight. 'Thank you,' he whispered. It seemed inadequate somehow.

But then the man spoke again, and his robotic voice sounded softer this time, more sympathetic. 'Ben, I need to talk to you about your father.'

He felt a chill cover his body.

'He's very ill, son. You know that, don't you?'

Ben nodded silently. He wasn't sure if he could bear to have this conversation.

'We don't know what this virus is yet. But we do know that it attacks the vital organs, starting with the lungs, then the blood, then the brain. Even the strongest people have difficulty withstanding such an attack. It's random, who survives and who doesn't.'

Ben lowered his eyes. It was clear what the man was trying to say. Half of him wished he would just spit it out; the other half didn't want to hear it.

And then the man was talking again. 'You need to prepare yourself, Ben . . .'

Ben closed his eyes.

'. . . prepare yourself for the fact that he might not be the same again.'

Ben blinked. Had he heard him right? 'You mean . . . ?' he faltered.

'It looks like your dad is going to pull through.' Ben's breath left him like an explosion. '*But* there's a possibility that he will be left severely disabled by his illness, Ben. The British Embassy in Kinshasa has been informed of his position, and they're sending transport back for you as soon as we've confirmed that neither of you are contagious any more. They've also contacted your mother, who is flying over to meet you both.'

'Can I see him?'

'Not yet. You both need to be isolated for a couple more days. But we're going to get you out of here as soon as we possibly can.'

Ben looked around him. 'What about everyone else?'

'They won't be so lucky, I'm afraid. The people who are immune to the virus will be kept isolated from the others. Those who succumb will be taken to the medical tent, where they'll receive our best attentions. Most of them won't make it.'

Ben's face became severe. 'There's a girl called Halima. I need to know how she is.'

'I'm sorry, Ben. I just don't have that information and we're going to keep you away from everyone else – so you can forget about seeing anyone apart from your dad. But you need to prepare for the worst – it's going to be pretty rough here, for a few months at least. A lot of people are going to die. But if we hadn't closed down this village and blocked up the mine in time, it could have been a million times worse. Word is, we've got you to thank for that.'

Ben averted his eyes. It seemed a hollow victory. 'I had a lot of help,' was all he could think of saying.

'Whatever,' the man from the UN replied. 'If anyone deserves to get out of here, it's you.'

He put a gloved hand on Ben's shoulder.

'We're going to get you home, son. We're going to get you home real soon.'

EPILOGUE

Two weeks later.

The private hospital room in Kinshasa was stark and white, and the sun shone brightly in through a small window. Russell Tracey was covered in a sheet, his head propped up on three plump pillows as he slept lightly. His breathing was heavy and measured, but it carried none of the frightening rasp of a couple of weeks ago.

At his bedside were two people, a boy and a woman. Ben Tracey had not been in the same room as his mother and father for years. It was weird, the three of them being there together now. Weird but nice – it was just a shame it had taken all this to make it happen. Bel had flown over the moment news of her son and ex-husband had reached her ears, and since she arrived, she and Russell hadn't even argued. Well, not much, anyway. Bel hadn't been able to resist a few arch 'I told you so's; but even she, with all her prophecies of doom, could never have predicted how their trip to the Democratic Republic of the Congo would end.

Most of the time, they all sat quietly, waiting for Russell's strength to return. Both Ben and his dad had been interviewed by the Kinshasa police, and there was quiet satisfaction to be had from the knowledge that Kruger and his associates were being dealt with by the authorities. But he had seen the corruption of this country first-hand – justice had a different way of working out here, and Ben didn't know if they would end up paying for what they had done. At least they would no longer be able to make money out of the suffering of the poor villagers, but he had no idea how well they had covered their tracks. He hoped they would be brought to book; but now, more than anything, he just wanted to go home.

Today, as Russell slept, Ben kept noticing the way his mum looked at her ex-husband. It's amazing how being close to death changes the way you look at the world, he thought to himself, and he began fantasizing whether this might be the beginning of something. Maybe he'd have a family once again.

He was interrupted from his daydream by a knock at the door – another nurse, no doubt. 'Come in,' Bel called – just like her to take charge, Ben thought with a smile. And his smile broadened when he saw who came through the door.

When he had last seen Halima, she had been dirty and bedraggled after everything they had been through. Before being given permission to leave the village, he had tried to persuade the UN doctors to let him see her, but that permission was flatly denied. He had been in isolation for days, and they weren't about to let him go back into infected areas. They wouldn't tell him what the result of her antibody test was; they wouldn't even tell him if she was dead or alive.

Now her hair was clean and her skin shining. Ben shot up from his seat. 'Halima!'

'They told me you would be here,' she replied with a grin.

'How are you? I mean, I didn't know if you—'

'They say I will not fall ill,' Halima said seriously. 'One of the men from the United Nations allowed me to travel back in a helicopter with him. I am staying with my sister.' She looked at Russell. 'How is your father?'

'He's OK. He's going to get better. Um . . . this is my mum.'

Bel stood up and politely shook Halima's hand. There was a smile on her face and a twinkle in her eyes. 'I've heard a lot about you, Halima,' she said mischievously.

Halima's eyes lowered and Ben found himself wanting to change the conversation. 'You heard about Abele?' he blurted out. He had no wish to upset Halima, but poor Abele had been on his mind ever since he left Udok.

Halima looked up, directly at him, and sadness shadowed her face. 'He was a strong man, but not strong enough.'

Ben shuddered as the image of the canvas-covered corridor leading to the incinerator slipped into his mind. Even now, weeks after his death, it didn't seem right that such a strong person should be laid low by a mere illness. It was wrong. 'He saved my life,' Ben said humbly. 'More than once. I can't believe he's . . .' Ben couldn't bring himself to say the word 'dead'.

'He is one of many,' Halima murmured. 'It will take many years for Udok to recover from this. Perhaps it never will.'

'I'm sorry, Halima.'

'You have nothing to be sorry about. I did not know Abele, though I will mourn him, more than I can say. But remember this: in saving your life, Abele saved the lives of many more. If it were not for you' – she looked over at Russell – 'and your father, of course, this evil virus might have spread. Then it would not only have been one village destroyed, but many.'

Ben looked sharply at her. 'So you believe it was a virus now?' he asked. 'Not a curse of the ancestors?'

Halima's face was inscrutable as she walked over to the window and looked out. 'Do you remember when we were in the forest? I told you that if a snake bites you, you may go to a doctor for a cure. But a doctor will not tell you why the snake bit you in the first place, or what it was doing in your house.'

Ben nodded silently, where a few weeks ago he might have scoffed.

'I believe that the ancestors punished us for disturbing their resting place. The manner in which they did it was up to them.'

Ben said nothing, but he felt inside his pocket. His fingers brushed against a small metal amulet that he had found round his father's neck. He had recognized it immediately. It was Abele's. Ben had intended to keep it as a memento but now, he thought, he had a better idea. He pulled it from his pocket and offered it to Halima. 'This was Abele's,' he said. 'He put it around my dad's neck when he was ill. I think you should have it.'

Halima looked at the token in Ben's outstretched palm, her face unreadable. Then she lifted her own hand and gently closed Ben's fingers back around the amulet. 'No, Ben. It brought your father great luck; maybe it will do the same for you. I have my own.' She touched her hand to her chest.

For a guilty moment, Ben found himself feeling glad that his father was asleep – no doubt he would have had a comment to make about such superstition. Come to think of it, he was surprised that his mum was keeping quiet and staring at him with an unknowable look on her face. Somewhere deep down, he was glad Halima had let him keep the token. Maybe it had had nothing to do with his dad's recovery, but then again . . .

Suddenly Halima's face grew less intense. 'My people have much to thank you for, Ben Tracey,' she told him seriously. 'And yet, perhaps, they do not know it. There are hard times ahead for Udok. Our livestock have been slaughtered, the mine is closed. Now there is no work for the men who remain, and little food. My village's problems, I think, are just beginning.'

Ben stared at her. 'But surely there will be help. The government, the United Nations . . .'

Halima smiled patiently. 'Humanitarian aid?' she said with irony in her voice. 'Yes, there will be some of that, for a while. But Udok's difficulties will soon be forgotten by the powerful people. Life in my village will be extremely difficult for many years to come.'

A cloud seemed to have descended on the room. 'Being a hero is not always easy, Ben Tracey.' Halima glanced apologetically at his mum. 'And now, you are with your family. I will not intrude any longer. But perhaps I will see you again one day?'

Ben stood up. 'I hope so,' he said sincerely.

Halima smiled modestly. She stepped up to Ben, put one hand on his arm, and kissed him lightly on the cheek.

'Goodbye, Ben,' she said.

Then she turned and left the room, closing the door quietly behind her.

Ben stared at the shut door for a few moments, strange emotions running through him. He touched his fingers to his cheek where Halima had kissed him. When he turned, his mum was watching him, one eyebrow raised and an amused look on her face.

'What?' he asked her defensively, acutely aware that he was beginning to blush.

'Nothing,' Bel said.

Her voice was heavy with meaning.

'Nothing at all.'

ALPHA FORCE

If you enjoyed this book, you'll also enjoy the *Alpha Force* series by Chris Ryan. Turn over to read the beginning of *Hunted*, which is also set in Africa.

PROLOGUE
THE DEAL

Families of elephants lifted their trunks, sniffing the air. In a rush of wind and thunder, the white belly of the plane roared overhead. The craft was flying at low altitude, looking for the landing strip. It sent buffalo pouring into the river. Herds of antelope, zebra and springbok scattered, startled, across the plains.

The plane skimmed the tops of the trees, beginning its final descent. The moment the wheels grazed the ground, the pilot stamped on the brakes. Dust rose up in hot ochre clouds.

The plane slowed to a halt just short of where the poachers waited with their battered Land Rover. There were three of them in combat fatigues, ammunition belts crossed over their shoulders. One had a scar in the brown skin of his cheek. The other two were white – one wore a hyena tooth set in silver on a chain around his neck; the other had a dirty yellow bandanna tied around his forehead.

They heard a noise among the trees and automatically levelled their weapons. A brown hyena trotted out of the bush, long fur topped by a tawny mane on its powerful shoulders. Its jaws were clamped around the bloody, torn-off leg of a wildebeest. The poachers lowered their weapons. They didn't expect any trouble in this remote part of the Zambian bush, but they weren't taking any chances. And you never knew – something might appear that was worth shooting.

The plane door opened. A slight figure got out and walked towards them. He had delicate oriental features; wisps of grey punctuated the jet-black hair. His lightweight, sand-coloured suit showed little creasing, despite the heat and the long journey he had made.

The poacher with the yellow bandanna reached behind into the Land Rover and pulled out a dusty sack. It was heavy. He needed both hands to lift it.

The oriental man put a hand out towards the sack. The diamonds on his Gucci watch glinted in the setting sun. He touched the bulging underside of the sack, feeling the shape of the contents. It wouldn't be the first time a poacher had tried to give him a live snake to take home instead of the goods he had paid for. His eyes betrayed no emotion.

'Show me,' he said.

The poacher kneeled down and tipped out the contents of the sack. Chunks of ivory tumbled onto the golden earth — giant hollow tusks sawn into pieces. Some of them were wide like sections of drainpipe, some were small like napkin rings. Many of the bigger pieces had bloody flesh clinging to them where they had been hacked out of the faces of elephants.

The buyer nodded and smiled. His face creased around his eyes like old tissue paper. While the poacher with the bandanna scooped up the ivory pieces and put them back in the sack, the other two fetched more from the jeep.

The buyer walked the short distance to the plane and came back with an envelope. He held it out. The poacher with the scar took it and counted it. Two thousand American dollars. He nodded to his companions.

The oriental man picked up the three sacks of ivory. Although they were heavy he carried them easily and loaded them into his plane. Then he turned to the poachers and said, 'I want more.'

'We're working on it,' replied the man with the scar, speaking in pidgin French as the buyer had. 'We'll be in contact.'

The oriental man nodded. He climbed into the passenger seat and buckled himself in. He leaned out to pull the door closed and had an afterthought. 'I'll pay you three thousand US dollars if you bring me a lionskin.'

1
TEAM ALPHA FORCE

Amber Middleton was out of the action and hating it. An ankle sprain suffered while training had put her on crutches, but much worse, it had forced her to pull out of the adventure race through Luangwa National Park, Zambia. She could have been spending three days running, mountain biking, abseiling and horse riding, pushing herself to the limits of endurance with her team-mates Alex, Li, Paulo and Hex. Just the first part alone was like a marathon – a fifty-kilometre run over savannah and into a river gorge. After that there would be more races, just as gruelling.

Gruelling, but fun. Right now, Amber wasn't having much fun. She was sitting in a striped deckchair beside the red Land Rover, wondering whether the neon-yellow bandage on her ankle was really the best colour to offset her ebony skin or whether she should have chosen the Day-Glo green option. Amber was having an easy time while her team-mates battled through a tough course. As well as physical exhaustion they also had to cope with sleep deprivation: the race was non-stop, twenty-four hours a day.

Amber didn't want to be sitting with her feet up, she wanted to be out on the course with her friends.

She was still involved in the race, but it was behind the scenes as the back-up crew with her uncle, John Middleton. They had to follow with vital equipment such as cycle helmets, climbing boots, running shoes, dry socks, medical supplies and food and drink. They dispensed these at transition points – large tents marking where one section of the race ended and another began. The transition point where Amber and John Middleton were waiting now marked the end of the cycling and the start of the hiking and abseiling.

A cluster of competitors appeared out of the dusty landscape. Amber looked up hopefully but it wasn't her team. Although everyone had set off on mountain bikes, this team were now on foot, pushing the bikes, two of the members leaning over the saddles, exhausted. They had slept for only a couple of hours during the thirty-six since the race began; the orange dust that covered them was like a fake suntan. 'Had to walk,' called one of the more awake ones cheerily. 'When I sat in the saddle I kept falling asleep.'

The teams and their back-up crews all wore name patches sewn onto their rucksacks and waterproofs. Amber had TEAM ALPHA FORCE proudly displayed on the front pocket of her shorts. She noticed a spot of mud on it and scratched it off with her fingernail. Never before had the name Alpha Force been seen in public; the five friends had used it only in the presence of a select few such as John Middleton.

Many of the teams in the race had formed just for the event and would disband afterwards, but Alpha Force were more enduring. They trusted one another, quite literally, with their lives. It had started when they were thrown together on a deserted island and had to escape a band of ruthless pirates. At the time, spoilt, beautiful Amber had been mourning her parents' death and hated the whole world. But then she discovered that her folks had had a secret life fighting human rights abuses. What she, Hex, Li, Alex and Paulo went through on the island was like a rebirth, and the five friends had vowed to carry on the Middletons' work. Alpha Force was born, and John Middleton became their anchor man, supplying them with finance and equipment.

The adventure race was an ideal training challenge for Alpha Force, a chance to pit their skills against the best endurance athletes in their age group. It also tested the bonds of a team to the limit. Each team had to finish together, so each member had to keep the others going when all they wanted to do was give up and sleep. Alpha Force were well prepared. As a matter of routine they trained together during every school break, so they functioned as a close-knit unit. When they scattered again to their various schools across the globe, they worked on their fitness and refined their individual skills. Alex lived in the north of England; Amber in Boston, Massachusetts; Paulo in Argentina; Hex in London; and Anglo-Chinese Li lived wherever her zoologist parents were posted.

In training for this event, Paulo had had them all to stay at his parents' ranch, where he had taught them how to handle their mounts both in the saddle and on the ground. Amber, already a keen horse-woman, had howled with laughter at Hex's first efforts. The London boy was a whiz with comput-ers and one of cyberspace's foremost hackers, but was baffled by an animal that completely ignored instructions to stop, go and turn.

Li, an expert in martial arts and free-climbing, had tutored them in abseiling skills during the same trip. Paulo took them to a canyon, and they had watched in awe as Li danced lightly down rock faces that seemed to go on for ever, oblivious to the dizzy-ing drop. Then she had climbed up again, light and sure-footed as a spider on a wall.

Running and cycling they all did every day to

maintain basic fitness, but the star in that department was Alex. Long-limbed and tall, he was built for endurance. Survival was in his blood: his father was a soldier in the SAS and Alex had inherited his relish for challenges in the roughest conditions.

Water sports were Amber's forte, and her privileged upbringing had enabled her to windsurf, water-ski and sail from an early age. Her navigation skills were second to none and would have been of great value in the race as the teams had to find their way from checkpoint to checkpoint through unknown canyons, across savannahs and rivers.

For the last few days of their stay in Argentina, Alpha Force had trained at night, mountain biking up the steep trails that overlooked the plains of Paulo's ranch, climbing, navigating through the endless open spaces, snatching sleep when they could. Then it was back to school for a few weeks, although they kept in e-mail contact to discuss their progress and general strategy for the event. Together Alpha Force were ready for anything the environment could throw at them.

But after all that preparation, Amber had tripped in a pothole while running and sprained her ankle. She had taken plenty of spills in her time and emerged with no more than bruises. This time, however, she had not even been able to get up. She had ripped several ligaments, and healing would take time. She couldn't believe her bad luck.

Amber watched as the other team were given coffee and equipment for the next part of the race. She went back to her book, a text on the languages of Africa. If she couldn't get in on the action, she would at least put the time to good use. Languages were another of her specialities, and she spent long hours studying them in her college library. At least she wasn't missing a real mission, she thought. The race wasn't work, it was play. It wasn't as if it would make a big difference to anyone's life at the end of the day. At least by resting now, she'd be fit and raring to go when a real mission came along.

Out of the corner of her eye she saw one of the competitors sit down and immediately fall asleep, like a robot whose batteries had run out. Even though she could see fatigue was overwhelming him, she felt a pang of envy.

Read the rest of *Alpha Force: Hunted*
to find out what happens!